Thunder Struck

A Pike Evans Trucking Adventure
Suz Eglington

You Create your own universe as you go

—Winston Churchill

Dead Women Walking

49'S THOUGHTS WHIRLED. *So, help me, God. I will kill her if she messes this up.*

He whooshed open the door, landing one foot inside as he let go of the handle. The sound of knives cutting against plates and the smell of sweet, smokey barbeque permeated the air.

His eyes scanned over the customers as he searched for Pike Evans. *Just my luck.* Wednesday night, crowded with families for early-bird specials. There was going to be a scene. He needed to avoid dinner and a show. He needed to find Pike quickly. Warn him what was coming.

He first found Clair, shifting her body as she leaned into Pike. Both wore black uniform T-shirts. Captain Jacobowski sat with her back to the door, engaged in a conversation with the man sitting next to her. *That must be Pike's dad.*

Clair smiled despite clearly disagreeing with Pike. Both stared in the direction of the table. She tilted her head, challenging him, pointing like she was suddenly right, slapping the table as she looked up and faced him like she was daring him to disagree. Both were now smiling wide at each other. Pike shook his head, leaning back and holding up Clair's phone as she swiped it from his hands, bumping her shoulder into his.

49 surveyed the layout of the tables, picking the quickest path through to them. Pike turned his head away from Clair as he spotted someone moving toward them. His eyes followed the outline of a man walking quickly, weaving through the tables.

Pike let out an audible exhale, releasing a deep breath that he hadn't realized he was holding. Relief washed over him at the sight of 49. *Finally, he's here.*

Pike turned to face Clair. "He made it," he said as he flicked his chin toward their previously missing team member. Pike got up quickly and Clair followed, pushing her chair back from the table as she stood.

Jacobowski turned her head and smiled, relaxing her shoulders. Not many people could draw out the captain's unguarded self, but he was one. Gus had finally made it. All was right at that moment.

She rose from her chair, stepping behind Kris as she decided how to sarcastically razz 49 about the last-minute business that took him away from the hanger. One of her favorite things in the world was bantering with Gus. He was the one man who really knew her.

49's stare locked onto Pike's expression like a camera lens pulling into focus. His mind raced, wondering how his news was going to change the kid's life once again.

Pike had already overcome one demon from his past. 49's gaze darted to Pike's sidearm. *That was one hell of a demon to overcome. He nearly didn't graduate because of it. Now this shitstorm pops up. This one might ruin his plans.*

49 continued to take in Pike's expression before his gaze turned to Clair. She was finally accepting Pike as her partner. They had bonded on a new level during the past week. He didn't know how they had broken that barrier, but they were committed to one another as a team. The best damn team he would ever pair up.

His eyes shifted back to Pike, who wore a relaxed expression and a lazy smile. *This is going to fuck up everything.*

49 clenched his jaw and made a silent vow. *I will make her disappear. She's not fucking up my future.* The words repeated over and over in his brain.

With only a few strides now between them, 49 rehearsed how to say it quickly so Pike could prepare. He had seconds to get this right. *Shit. Just tell the kid. Straight up, no chaser.*

Pike shifted his focus to his dad, still seated at the end of the table. Captain Jacobowski smiled at Kris and angled her body toward him as the two spoke. Pike's grin spread wider as he took in a subtle, proud inhale. His chest swelled out as his eyes swept over his group. This was his family. This was where he belonged.

Clair nodded proudly, admiring him. He was hers, deep down. He just needed to toughen up some more. She could mold him to what she wanted. That much she was sure of.

Pike wanted her to step closer, wanted to put his arm around her. She was going to be his. He knew she would figure it out and he was willing to give her all the time she needed. The age thing was bullshit. She was only five years older. Besides, her ex, Jon Hanskon, was aging out, and Pike had never felt as strong as he felt now, growing more confident and physically fit than ever before. She would see that as a plus. It would be attractive. That's the kind of guy she was into.

Making agent was the first step. A giant accomplishment for him. One of the biggest. It was right up there with when he was a teenager, when he flipped his uncle's tractor trailer on its side and his uncle made him upright it all by himself. It had taken him the entire night, but come morning that damn trailer was wheels down, where they ought to be.

But becoming an agent, this was gold. No way could his mother tell him there was no good life in trucking anymore, even though it had already paid for the house she was living in and a lot of other properties Kris owned outright. Finally, a job Pike loved and grew up in. Back out on the road, hauling whatever the government would tell him to deliver. Pike's happiest memories were on the road with his dad and uncle growing up.

Everyone Pike wanted close in his life was here to celebrate his new job.

Turning to greet 49, Pike watched the expression on the old man's face harden with each step closer. Pike's lighthearted feeling vanished.

Something was wrong. He could sense it through 49's eyes, making his pulse quicken as his stomach knotted. Did something happen to the guys? Cory, LaRue, Vonn? His gut twisted again and he stiffened.

Clair glanced up. She could see the change in his expression, feel his panic. She stepped closer to him. He needed her. She knew it. She leaned her head toward 49.

49's words hushed as he stopped less than two feet from them, his arm extended awkwardly as he began trying to explain. Pike instinctively reached out to him, concerned that 49 needed help. Maybe he was reading this all wrong.

It was 49 who cupped Pike's elbow first. "Brace yourself. Take a breath, kid. Let's look on the bright side."

Pike scrunched up his face, unable to follow what 49 was saying.

49 continued, "There is an explanation."

Clair's hand rested on Pike's back. He relaxed, letting her know the contact was welcome. He wanted to do the same to her. What the hell was 49 going on about? He liked that Clair was just as concerned. They were in this together. Her eyes shifted from 49 to Pike. Whatever this was, she would be there for him. They were a team. Nothing could stand in their way.

49 turned his head to look back at the entrance as he spoke to Pike, who interrupted the babbling words that were coming out of 49. Pike and Clair launched into a series of questions. Nothing made any sense.

Pike shifted his body to search over 49's shoulder, his eyes now fixated on the front door. His jaw dropped.

Dead. She was supposed to be dead. How was it then, that Jackie now stood in the doorway of the BBQ restaurant? A theory that she was abducted by aliens carried solid weight. Pike convinced himself that was the reason for her disappearance from social media. She lived by her posts. That was her life. Then the storm hit. She vanished. Nothing.

It didn't make any sense. How could she be here? In this restaurant. At his graduation celebration.

Pike slowed his breathing, but he was losing the battle to keep calm. His heart pounded inside his chest like a paintball gun set to automatic fire. His upper-arm muscles tightened and he became suddenly aware of his stiffening spine.

Pike could feel the light pressure from each of Clair's fingers pressing into him. His lower-back muscles locked and his chest and stomach constricted with every memory of Jackie that surfaced in his head. First the photos of Jackie kissing other men. An uneasiness fluttering throughout. He couldn't move. His eyes burned into her standing at the entrance.

Four days ago, lightning had walloped Pike's house, where Jackie temporarily lived. The blow hit so forceful that it split the house four ways. Four ways, like giving a two-year-old a crowbar to cut a birthday cake. He had seen the initial pictures from when the demolition crew first arrived.

Thoughts plagued him for days as he imagined her death inside the house. The only other possibility Pike dared to consider was an abduction. Not by anything on this earth.

The mysterious cargo he had been transporting. There was more truth to alien lifeforms than almost anyone knew. They are real. There are other beings in the universe that are exploring Earth.

Pike's new job presented him with more than enough proof. Very strange occurrences were happening on a regular basis now.

Pike had even seen one for himself just a week prior when a massive bolt of what seemed like sentient lightning attacked him and his crew in the hanger.

His veins hummed as the memory resurfaced. He could feel tiny zaps on his skin, almost like pins poking him all over. Pike quickly glanced down his arm, raising it with a strange feeling. He wiped his hands over the spot and rubbed the feeling away.

Clair could feel Pike stiffen. She had sensed this from him every time Hanskon had arrived unannounced, but what was happening now? Why wasn't 49 saying more? He was talking but leaving a lot of information out.

Clair watched as Pike stretched out his fingers and then quickly closed them into to a fist. She could feel heat. His body temperature was practically radiating from him. She lowered her hand from his backside. Yes, heat. He was cooking.

Clair blinked, not sure what was happening. The air surrounding him seemed to blur. There was an odd contrast that was visible. Clair reached out to grab his upper arm and stopped midway. She could feel Pike's sudden shift from anger to concern, so much so that her eyes abandoned him and turned toward the door.

That was Jackie. She was seeing what Pike was feeling. Jackie stood still at the entrance. Clair was certain it was her, even though she had only seen that one picture on his phone.

Pike lifted his eyes and turned toward Clair, who was staring at Jackie. He repeated in a whisper, "I can't believe it," more to himself than to be heard by others. Clair reached to stop him. He turned his head, wide-eyed eyebrows shifting up and down as questions assaulted his brain. He nodded to Clair. "It's okay."

She released her grip, knowing and feeling what Pike was going through. The questions in his head, his all-too-familiar moment of hope. It was that feeling she had felt all those times Hanskon had come back to her. Clair studied Jackie. *Where has she been? How did she find him? How did she get here? How is she still alive?*

Pike snapped out of his trance, zipping past 49 as he darted toward Jackie. His mind raced with explanations. *The explosion from lighting hitting the house was a cover-up. They said no one could have survived.* He was banking on this. He had wanted to believe she was abducted into another world. Alive. Somehow safe.

Nothing about the unknown was safe. Aliens. Little green men. Or, in his personal experience, a glowing inchworm-type thing that could mimic volts of energy and threw nasty temper tantrums.

Pike had even felt the little guy when he met it just over two weeks ago. He was certain he could feel it now. There was a connection he had with the nasty little bugger. He could still feel something that he couldn't explain to anyone, like this strange hum happening right now inside of him. He knew something wasn't normal, but he felt so strong, so healthy.

Humans are not the only lifeforms in the universe. Those bright white energy orbs, gazillion-watt surges that came in the form of lightning, had proven it to Pike and the crew that was present that night. Even Cooper was convinced.

Pike watched Jackie's silhouette standing still in the entrance. His brain fought to tell him it wasn't her. It was a local girl. A lookalike. A local who only resembled the looks of Jackie, because his Jackie would never wear a simple summer dress and sandals. Damn, it looked good on her. Loose fit, but still showing off her shapely figure.

This was the Jackie that Pike would have considered marrying. Someone to play house with, to take care of him. To dress like this. Other parts of Pike began to liven up.

The memory of Jackie taking care of him during their first month together warmed his heart. Just like how his mother always envisioned the way a family should function. Not living on the road all those early years. Memories from his childhood shifted energy in his head. All he knew and ever wanted was a truck-driving life. It was where he belonged. Pike and the road. Clair understood it. 49 was heading for retirement from a driving career. His dad Kris was semi-retired and living large from a driving career. His mother hated living on the road. Jackie wouldn't have liked it either.

He could feel his body temperature rising much hotter than normal and couldn't understand why sweat wasn't rolling off of him. Nothing. Instead, he was as dry as the desert.

He moved quickly, cutting around chairs and zig-zagging between tables to get to her. He didn't hesitate until he fumbled around the last corner, catching his balance from clipping his foot against a seat, slowing his pace as he walked the final few feet before finally stopping directly in front of her. Why couldn't this have happened tomorrow? He and Clair were flying back to Massachusetts to deal with the mess. One day. Why couldn't Jackie have just shown up tomorrow? Not right here with his trucking family.

People were missing from his first run. More than 150 passengers had vanished from the plane that Pike, 49, and Clair delivered to Colorado. That number now included two missing patrol officers who harassed them that night. The two officers who touched the plane and set of glowing marching ants all over the tarp of Clair Morris's cargo.

Vonn Nash from Team One of the Colorado Highland Yetis was keeping track of the disappearances. Pike figured Jackie had been taken when he tried to make nice with the stowaway volt on their flight back to Bragg. He blinked. Jackie was now making eye contact. A shiver zipped through his right side. It was her. Alive. Standing there in flesh and blood.

All deals were off. *Even the aliens didn't want her. Damn those aliens.*

Jackie waited in the doorway while wearing the perfect dress. She would fit right in down here. No one could come in or go out without asking her to move. That's how real she was, standing there blocking the entrance.

Her hand strategically wiped what looked like tears rolling down her face. She cupped her hands together, covering her mouth and nose as the tears redirected, streaming along her index finger on her left side. Pike could see her managing a weak smile under her hands. He reached out, touching her hands, guiding them down and away from her face as she squeaked out, "Hi," trying to swallow to regain some composure. She cleared her throat a few times.

Her face tilted down shyly, now heating with red blotches as if she were embarrassed.

Pike moved his hands up, controlling the shaking deep in his core. He remained steady on the outside, quickly cupping each of her shoulders. He needed contact with her. He needed to feel that she was the real deal.

Her slender frame relaxed in his grip. He gently squeezed, once more making sure that she was not an illusion. She flinched and he relaxed his grip. Something interrupted his thoughts, as if his brain was just hijacked. It was as though Clair was asking the words in his ear standing next to him, only she wasn't. She was waiting back by their table. Even so he could feel her thoughts. He heard her voice in his head, *Get the facts. Get the facts. Where has she been since Saturday and why haven't you heard from her? Why is she here now? Why is she here?*

Pike's heart was pounding. Her eyes were wet and soft, as if she was saying she loved him and she wanted to work it out between them. All he could do was admire how pretty she looked in this sundress. Pike took in her smell from the body spray she used. It was new, or at least he didn't remember this one. How she felt under his touch scrambled all his senses. His ears heard her say "Hi" softly. It wasn't enough. His brain and heart were in a boxing match, duking it out.

His knees bent and he nearly buckled to the ground. Pike wasn't sure he was in total control of his muscles. There was a strange energy inside. He could sense his body reacting. He instinctively kept his hands on her shoulders while his brain concentrated on the tension, grip, her breath, and his own heartbeat and chest expanding with each inhale. Something inside made him focus on controlling his overt reaction. His mind had begun winning the fight over his heart.

Slowly, she lifted her eyes and let them rake over his changed physique. He was bent down to her height as their eyes met. "Jackie?"

She pressed her lips together, then let them part, blowing out a breath. "Pike . . . you look . . . good."

Pike held her firmly in place. It didn't matter. She wasn't going anywhere. He continued to scan every part of her. Skin, arms, hands, torso, toes. Her toenails painted a light pink. Her favorite color nail polish. He knew this intimate fact about her. She had sent him to the local pharmacy many times to pick up her favorite shades. His eyes softened as they focused on her pink toes, and a slight grin edged up the corner of his mouth. That was the shade he would have brought home. He glanced back upward, meeting her eyes once more, then quickly looked over her shoulder.

Dirt cluttered the air as a car rolled past in the background. The crunching sound of gravel beneath tires alerted Jackie and she turned her head, forgetting that she was still in the doorway.

Other restaurant patrons were here and parking. She and Pike watched the family's commotion, from the car doors slamming to the mother instructing her children to watch out for cars and that they had better behave. They were loud enough, making this moment between Pike and Jackie more urgent. Jackie rotated her head back to face Pike, wearing a softened smile.

Her hair was shiny, healthy, hanging down freely. This was the way Pike always liked it styled. There was not one mark on her that he could see. Finally, he pulled her into him, lining her body against his, wrapping his arms around her tight. She exhaled with relief and pressed the side of her head into his chest. She wrapped her arms around him as she declared, "I missed you so much, baby." Wrapping tight around him. *My gun!* He panicked, holding it all inside. She was at an advantage and had access to his gun. And yet he felt so different, so strong. He could sense every movement her frame was making. She let out a hum, holding him close.

Pike's emotions spiked and dropped with every passing second. He was grateful that she was okay, but also irritated that she had shown up here.

"I can't believe it. You're here?"

His thoughts and gaze turned back toward Clair, who was watching the two of them. Her face tightened. She was staring hard.

The family approaching from across the lot shouted back and forth to one another as the kids ran toward the entrance.

Clair abandoned her personal feelings and cleared her throat before maneuvering around the table. Pike might need her.

49 caught her by the forearm. "Let them have a minute."

Her eyes burned into his hand on her arm, halting her forward momentum. She was shocked that he had stopped her.

Clair needed to ground herself. This was stupid. There was no reason to be angry with 49. She took in a breath, resisting the arm to shake free from his grip. She forced herself to mimic 49's concerned expression as she relaxed her arm.

Still, Clair didn't want to give them a minute. She knew what was going to happen. She wished someone had reminded her about the truth that people don't change. Jackie had been a troublemaker for the past two weeks. 49 didn't know much about it because Pike had only opened up to her. Not him.

Clair's thoughts ping-ponged. If she went to Pike now, what would it accomplish right at this moment?

She studied Pike as he held Jackie, his body aligned with hers. He looked protective. But even worse, he looked happy. Clair's stomach twisted into a knot.

Heat flamed up through the back of her neck and spread to her ears, which itched from the burn. Her eyes suffered at Jackie's victorious expression, her face resting against Pike's chest. Smug. A stupid, I've-got-you-now grin.

Jackie's eyes were closed. Clair swept her gaze down over her posture. She was up on her tip-toes, and suddenly her arms were letting go of the hold she had on Pike. Just her hands rested on the outside of his shoulder blades right now as she began to lift her face off his chest.

Pike also broke their connection, glancing around the restaurant as he separated himself from Jackie. They were still blocking the door.

His hand turned her away from where his gun rested at his side, and from Clair, as he stepped forward, guiding Jackie outside while holding the door for an incoming family.

Clair could no longer see Pike. She assumed he wanted to talk with Jackie outside. *Maybe he has some sense after all? Probably not.* Clair turned her body to head toward the restroom and away from everyone to pull herself together and bury her thoughts. The last thing she wanted to be was obvious. Especially around 49.

49 watched her disappear behind the ladies' room door and turned his attention back to the rest of the party. He angled his body to meet Kris, but his eyes were locked on Captain Jacobowski. He watched the facial expression she directed at him as she tried to figure out what was going on. She kept glancing back at Kris, with a sudden polite grin appearing and disappearing as she quickly refocused on 49, distracted by his obvious unease.

49 finally acknowledged Kris when he heard the man telling a story about Pike outsmarting a gang of bootleggers when he was just 15 years old. 49 perked up at the word "bootlegger." His expression became even more bewildered. *No! It couldn't be!?* Were his eyes playing tricks on him? *No! What in God's name?*

49 studied the man. His jaw, head shape, nose, were the same as he remembered. Same eyebrows. He always kept his eyebrows and facial hair neat. This guy's hair was lighter, more salt and less pepper. Not quite all gray. Some dark strands still held firm. His height fit the profile, too, about five foot seven, possibly shorter.

49, standing at least five inches taller than the man, craned his neck down to look more closely. "Hank? You're ..." *It couldn't possibly be ...*

Kris's protective stare met 49's eyes. *Jesus Christ.* It was him. 49 was experiencing his second ghost sighting of the day.

Kris moved forward, guiding 49 back a few steps and angling his body sideways and dropping his voice so Captain Jacobowski couldn't hear as he corrected 49. "It's Kris. My name is Kris now." Kris stepped away with a cautious smile.

49's watchful eyes took in Kris's full appearance. "I don't understand? How? ... What?"

Kris reached out and playfully slapped 49 on his upper arm, "Story for another day. This isn't the time or the place."

49 mouthed, "Kris?"

He nodded. "Small world, isn't it? What I want to know is how did you find my boy?"

49 compressed his lips pushing a breath through his nose that even Kris heard. Pike must have taken after his mother. 49 didn't see the family resemblance from Hank's side. Pike was also a half a foot taller.

Of all the restaurants in all the United States, today, here was Hank Domings standing right here in front of 49, more than thirty years after disappearing.

When Pike had first mentioned Wade Doming, 49 couldn't believe he was really Wade's nephew. Pike didn't even know Wade was blood, instead speaking of him like an old family friend. But Wade really was Pike's uncle after all. Why the cover-up?

49 had convinced himself it was all a coincidence, that Kris was just some random trucker who had hooked up with Wade working for a private company. It was possible. Unlikely, but possible.

Wade was a personable guy. A thief, but friendly folk. The best damn driver he 49 ever met. Better than himself. He could picture Wade teaching Pike how to drive. He probably put the kid to the test every single time.

Picturing it now, 49 had to admit that Pike drove just like that son of a bitch. *Damn.* Why hadn't he picked up on that earlier?

Thirty years had passed, but Kris wore the same slicked-back hair. Same daring twinkle in his eye.

"Your boy found me," 49 explained. "I was having an issue while driving a heck of a load. Medication fell out of reach."

Maggie took in their conversation and then stopped them, pointing a finger at Gus. "I shouldn't be listening to this. Excuse me, gentlemen."

She stepped away and Kris turned to her, nodding out of politeness with a smile as she headed for the restroom. Kris motioned for 49 to sit down. "Ooh wee, that's a fine-looking lady! If they had personnel like that back in the day, Wade would have stuck around. No wonder you're still here."

A waitress stopped at their table. "Anything I can get you, gentlemen?"

49 flipped his coffee mug upright. "Coffee, miss."

She smiled. "Sure thing. More iced tea, sir?" She pointed to Kris's glass.

"Just bring a pitcher, sweetheart. A few of us are drinking."

She nodded. "One pitcher of iced tea and a coffee. Be right back."

They watched her walk away. Kris flipped his head up. "You were saying?"

"Captain Jacobowski is out of your league, Hank. Besides, she's your kid's boss."

"Kris. Call me Kris."

"Say, how did you become Kris?"

Kris peered around. "Here is the quick version. Between Pike's mother and the damn law, Hank needed to disappear."

Clair headed back to their table and quickly glanced at the entrance, finding Pike still absent. Both men eyed her. As she approached the table, 49 straightened up and Kris standing up out of his seat. "You don't have to do that, Mr. Evans," she said. "I appreciate it, but not necessary."

"My momma would disagree. Let's just say I don't go against how I was raised."

She nodded. "Old-school southern hospitality. You are a rare breed, Mr. Evans. Never seen your son execute those fine manners, though. Apparently, they stopped with you."

"Pike was raised by his mother, for the most part. Yankee women are . . . Well, let's just leave it at that. Please, call me Kris."

Clair shifted to 49. "I take it that's Jackie out there? What's the story?"

Kris looked over his shoulder. "You found the girl? The one who blew up my house?"

49 sighed. "She left Saturday before the storm hit. Made her way down here. Blombach found her snooping around the base this morning, thinks she might have been here last night. There was an incident over at the hotel. See anything unusual?"

Clair assaulted 49 for answers. "How did she get here? Does she have Pike's car? What about her phone? Why hasn't he been able to get in touch with her?"

"Yes, she has his car. She left her phone behind. I'm sure there are a lot of questions. Let's not overwhelm the girl just yet."

"That's why he couldn't reach her?! She left it behind? Traveling to North Carolina without a phone? She's never been here. Wasn't that convenient of her?"

"Packed a bag and just left is what I got out of the conversation coming down here. She didn't tell anyone. Says she needed to get away from that life back in Agawam."

Clair sat back. Her face tightened. Even those few sentences confirmed Jackie was a liar and manipulative. The sound of the fans overhead made her look upward, displeased, giving her a chance to think things over while taking a moment watching the whirling blades.

She replied slowly, drawing out each letter, "G-r-e-a-t." This wasn't her battle. Pike needed to stand firm. She shook her head slowly, pressing her lips together. She knew he would cave.

The waitress poured 49's coffee and returned with the iced tea, placing the pitcher at the end of the table along with a bowl filled with sugars and creamer and a basket of fresh-baked rolls.

Maggie returned to the table to find Pike still missing. Kris stood up again and stayed that way until she was seated. She motioned toward 49 and jabbed playfully, "I see we have one gentleman at our table."

49 grumbled. "I'm still recovering."

Kris leaned in, eyes inquisitive yet concerned. He and 49 had a past no matter how much Kris wanted to bury it. "Recovering?"

Clair lifted her hand, cupping 49's shoulder. "Surgery last week. Probably good for you to move around and not sit for too long." She glanced down at his coffee cup, knowing he was breaking the doctor's orders.

She flicked her chin at his cup. "Hope that's decaf, Boss. I'm telling Pike if it isn't."

49 scowled. "Too many Chiefs not enough Indians around here. Don't you start on me."

Pike returned, walking ahead with Jackie following. His shoulders hung low, head pointed down. He looked defeated, wiped out, like every ounce of energy had been drained from his soul. His eyes watching where he was going instead of the people waiting for him at the table. Clair shifted, ready to leap out of her chair.

Pike tried to make sense of his thoughts. Why was she here? Right now? It didn't make sense. His eyebrows scrunched together.

Clair observed his body language as Pike walked closer. She now had a clear view of Jackie. His supposed-to-be-dead ex-girlfriend was alive and interfering where she didn't belong. Here. Right here in North Carolina. She did not belong here.

Clair knew his mind was far away from her. Damn Jackie for showing up right now. Clair wanted to make this right. Despite having spent only the past month together, Clair would have bet anyone that she knew Pike better than this soul-sucking skank. Jackie was nothing more than a lifetime of bad decisions, and probably a lot of credit card debt.

Pike was still going over the past four days. After he got the new that his dad's house had blown up, he was assigned to pick up and deliver what was left of his family home for observation, and he hadn't been right ever since. No word from Jackie to ease his mind.

He and Clair had delivered the rubble to the Virginia facility. It was one of the East Coast sites that studied the aftermath of unusual occurrences. Pike was sure Jackie had been abducted by the alien that found them on the flight back from Colorado. The idea had consumed his thoughts. Otherwise, she would have contacted him. She must have heard what happened to the house.

Nothing. There hadn't been so much as a word from any of her friends to say she was alive and still here. But here was Jackie, walking behind Pike, very alive, and looking beautiful. There wasn't a single scratch on her. Clair doing a thorough scan of all the skin Jackie was showing. She tore her eyes away, looking down at her own uniform, then back at Pike. At least they matched.

Jackie followed Pike right to the table, stopping behind him perfectly groomed, wearing light makeup and a yellow-and-white thigh-length floaty sundress with brown sandals. She had clearly planned this meeting, right down the gold ankle bracelet. Jackie was definitely more put together than Pike at this moment. Damn it. This was Pike's day.

Clair wasn't happy about this intrusion on their graduation party. Why couldn't she have stayed away for one more day? Just one more day alone with Pike would have made all the difference.

49 remained in his seat. Clair made no sign of giving up her position next to him. Pike stopped at the end of the table and hesitantly dragged one hand up, palm, facing the ceiling, as he gestured toward Jackie and introduced her to the group. He kept his gaze focused firmly on the table throughout, avoiding eye contact with everyone. He gestured with his hand as he continued, vaguely introducing them as father, captain, boss, and, coming to Clair, introducing her as his partner. Clair smiled wide.

49 scanned the seating arrangements. This was Pike's Day. He wanted him to feel like they still had his back no matter who showed up. 49 started to move to accommodate the new guest, but Pike shot his hand out. "No, stay, sir. I will sit next to Clair. Jackie can sit next to Captain Jacobowski across from me."

Clair reluctantly offered to give up her seat. Since 49 had offered, so should she. It was the right thing to do. "I can move."

Pike insisted. "No." He guided Jackie to sit next to Jacobowski. The captain studied Pike's expression. He was rattled. She didn't want to add to his uneasiness. He had already overcome a great deal in the past month. This was his celebration party. She nodded neutrally. "Hello Jackie."

Jackie leaned in, whispering in Pike's ear. "But I don't know anyone here. Why can't I sit next to you?"

Pike pulled her chair out, motioning for her to sit. He glanced at Captain Jacobowski with a forced grin. "Thank you, Captain." He walked around the table, taking the seat next to Clair, who was taking another long look at Jackie. *This girl is pretty*, she thought. *Empty, but pretty*.

Jackie reached over the table to hold Pike's hand. He pulled it away and she shyly smiled as she retracted.

That was the sign Clair had waiting for. Full confirmation. She needed to protect Pike. She now knew exactly how he felt about Jackie showing up. Clair understood this emotion. She had to come to terms with this same feeling for the past two and a half weeks with Hanskon inviting himself to Yeti Team One's training operation. Her stomach has been in knots from the moment she saw his jeep racing toward the plane until the night Pike was hazed.

She knew this feeling. She and Pike had more in common than they both realized.

The waitress returned and Jackie what she wanted to drink. She requested cola with plenty of ice. Pike inquiring if they carried beer, glancing around for a sign of branding, beer logos on the walls or bottles on the tables.

She nodded. "Of course," and listed what they had to offer.

Beer was beer to Pike. The visit with Clair's father was the last time he had even seen one. "Bud Light, thank you."

Clair raised her hand. "Make that two."

Pike stole a quick glance at Clair. She moved her arm, lining it up against his left arm. When she made contact, he didn't pull away. "This is a celebration, right?" She pressed her shoulder into his as she smiled, reassuring him that everything was going to be okay.

Kris raised his glass. "My boy is finally taking his life back from his mother. He's an agent now. Agent Evans. I can't believe you stumbled into this . . ." He paused ever so slightly, realizing Captain Jacobowski was part of the operation.

It had been thirty years since his brother had been fired from this cover-up operation. Kris shifted his gaze to Pike, who raised one eyebrow. The right side of Kris's mouth curled slightly as he finished his sentence, ". . . this program. Tell me son, how did you find out about G.H.O.S.T.?"

Pike rubbed his chin and sat forward. He broke contact with Clair's arm and a shiver replaced the warmth instantly. A quick rub and the tingle was gone. He tilted his head hard to the left. There was no stopping the sly grin that was spreading across his face as he looked first to Clair, then at Captain Jacobowski. The way Kris hesitated to describe G.H.O.S.T. signaled he knew all about this division.

Pike leaned over, catching 49's attention. He wasn't sure what information he could share, and instead waited for 49 to say something first.

Watching everyone speak, Jackie realized she was the only one at the table who didn't know about Pike's new job. She asked Pike directly, "What ghost? What is that? Are you working with real ghosts?"

Captain Jacobowski stopped the conversation. "It's just an acronym, Jackie. Might I remind everyone that we are in the company of civilians. Let's save the shop talk for the shop."

Jackie was confused. "What's an acro . . . What did you call it?"

Clair quickly answered, "Acronym. You know, 'OMG,' that's an acronym."

Jackie's eyes widened and her tone turned snarky. "That's texting language."

Clair leaned forward, matching Pike's body language. Pike bumped her with his elbow and answered Jackie more politely, "OMG is the acronym for 'oh my god.' G.H.O.S.T. is the shorter name for what we do."

"What do you do?"

"Transportation. Government transportation."

She smiled. "I bet it pays more?"

Pike stared, pissed she had said that in front of all his colleagues.

Kris sat back. "I know all about your racket."

Captain Jacobowski turned to Kris, curious that he put that right out there for conversation. She knew a lot of truckers had their own theories of what G.H.O.S.T. was. Not many actually knew what it really was about. "Perhaps this topic should be tabled for another time."

Kris caught her tone and respected her request. He leaned back in his chair, catching a look at the back of Jackie's head, admiring her salon-dyed golden locks. "Pike, this the girl who blew up my house?"

Jackie went from slumping over to sitting erect in a flash. "What?! What happened? Did something happen to the house?"

Kris sat forward. He didn't seem to buy her act. Pike defended her by explaining that there was a possibility she didn't know what had happened. "The house is gone. Something happened Saturday. That's what I was trying to tell you in the parking lot before you started crying."

Her shoulders slumped forward again. She sounded like everyone was ganging up on her. "I left my phone behind. I told you how much I wanted to get out of there. I needed to leave that life, Pike. Start new. New place, just like here, just for us. Our new life together. We need this. You know that."

Pike shrugged, ignoring everything she said except for the part about her phone. "Probably not your best decision. What if something had happened to my car?"

Clair was curious. "How did you find your way down here? How did you know he would still be here?"

"I wrote directions when Pike told me where he was. I've been wanting to come down here for three weeks, but he said I couldn't."

Clair continued to mimic Pike's posture, bringing her hand up to rub her chin. "Get caught in that severe storm?"

"It was just a storm. Like any storm. Nothing to worry about."

Clair didn't like Jackie. "Really? That's odd. They had travel advisories all up the East Coast."

"Didn't bother me. I was thinking about Pike."

Kris leaned over, still not buying this act she was putting on. "That was risky. Traveling in a storm, leaving your phone behind. Needed a quick getaway? Kind of makes me think there was some foul play involved with my house blowing to smithereens?"

Tears filled her eyes. "Pike? I didn't do anything but leave."

Kris pressed her. "Leave the gas on from the stove?"

She shot out of her chair, defending herself. "I don't touch the stove."

Pike showed his amusement by flexing an eyebrow, certain she wasn't lying this time. "That's true. Jackie doesn't cook."

Pike motioned, pointing his index finger at her chair for her to sit back down. Her tear-stained eyes darted around the table to find everyone focused on her. "I didn't. Why would he say that, Pike?"

Pike leaned forward. "He's kidding. Sit."

The waitress returned with Jackie's soda and their two beers. Clair watched her place them on the table. "Perfect timing. Thank you."

Kris picked up his iced tea, rattling the ice around. "She's gonna need to be cleared by the authorities."

He leaned back, talking to Jackie behind Captain Jacobowski's back. "Goldilocks, you should have stayed missing for another week until they wrote me that check."

He sat forward again as he spoke to Pike. "This is going to cause a delay with the insurance paperwork." He huffed out, "I don't like delays with trucks, people, or paperwork."

Jackie stood again, stepping away from her seat. She turned, crying as she scurried around tables and chairs toward the restaurant's entrance.

Pike stood. "Jackie, wait! Dad, can't this wait until later? I don't need this right now."

"Better go get her, son. We can't have her getting away now that we know she's accounted for."

Pike shuffled after her. 49 added, "Good point. Didn't know there was propane involved. It makes a lot of sense, the way the house fragmented."

His coffee smelled of simple comforts. He took a sip, thoughts going back to the gas stove. "I don't know the girl. Morris, you have been with Evans continually. Did he talk about her at all? Do you think she is capable of such a malicious act?"

Kris wanted to know the answer as well. He encouraged her to speak. "Pike told me he kicked her out almost a month ago. He specifically used the terminology *kicked her out*. I don't know how well you know my boy, but he's gotta be fairly worked up to get that kind of reaction from him."

Clair nodded. "He's a marshmallow."

Kris brought his hands down on the table loudly. "No idea where he gets that from. His mother comes from a strong line of overreactors."

He glanced up at 49, knowing he was going to get a response from what he was about to say next. "I've been guilty of handling situations wrongly. Possibly a touch of overreactions in my bloodlines too."

49 chuckled. "Understatement."

Captain Jacobowski watched Gus and Kris. "Excuse me? Do you two know each other?"

Kris sat back, pulling his iced tea toward the edge of the table. "A million lifetimes ago."

Clair glanced from 49 to Kris as her leg started bouncing under the table. "You guys know each other?"

49 cocked his head. "Story for another day."

She wasn't letting it go like Captain Jacobowski did. "Did you know Pike? I mean, when he first arrived?"

"Nope. Sheer coincidence. New meaning to small world. However, I did know *this* punk thirty-something years ago."

He held his coffee cup with two hands. The world just got a little smaller. "Tell me, was anything else in the house propane, or just the stove?"

Kris sipped the tea and smacked his lips. "Just the stove. Never liked cooking on an electric range." He placed his tea back down on the table. "The way I see it, that girl needs to be questioned. I reckon someone investigating will want to know she's surfaced. My ex-wife said she stole money right out of her purse a few months ago." Everyone shook their head to some degree.

Clair didn't like Jackie even before she had met her. Now it was evident this girl needed to go. Kris lifted his tea again, pointing to Clair. "Pike has a soft heart when it comes to people in need."

She nodded. "Clearly." She then addressed 49, "She's using him. Kittrick, he did open up to me about her."

Kris's eyes shifted to 49. "That's what the ex-wife says. She's using him. I kind of suspected it when he let her back in while down here training. I try to stay out of the female relations with him. Lord knows I've been misguided myself. He's going to learn through experience, just like the rest of us."

Clair added, "You're right. He doesn't know how to deal with it. You are capable of giving advice, aren't you? I would think he would listen to his father."

She lifted her phone to read a text.

Kris pointed. "You young kids don't go anywhere without your phones."

Clair put hers down. "True. How convenient she left hers behind."

Captain Jacobowski began to stand and Kris stood up with her. "Ma'am?"

She extended her hand. "I have to head back."

Kris faced her, caressing the back of her hand with his thumb as he held it. "That's a shame. You haven't even had anything to eat yet."

She pulled her hand back. "You have a fine son, Mr. Evans. He is going to be a fine agent."

"He's still young," he admitted, "but one hell of a driver."

She improvised her smile. "I've seen what you mean. It was a pleasure to meet you." She nodded a goodbye at 49 and Clair.

Pike stood in the parking lot with Jackie sobbing into his shoulder when he saw Captain Jacobowski walk past. "You're leaving, captain?"

She sympathetically nodded. "Congratulations, Evans. I'll see you Monday."

Jackie hid as she held onto Pike, burying her face into his chest until she finally began to quiet down. Pike's thoughts were on his dad, Clair, and 49 sitting inside. This was his graduation dinner and she was ruining it.

"You believe me, Pike, don't you? I just wanted to leave that life behind."

"Jackie, pull yourself together. I'm glad nothing happened to you. Look, dad's right. We're going to have to go back and get you cleared. I don't want my parents to have any reason to think you did this. Dad is staying the night. I have the next four days off. We can go back and get this whole thing sorted out and then figure everything out, okay?"

He tilted her chin up and raised his eyebrows while he waited for her to answer. Her big eyes said she believed he would get her through this. She squeaked out, "Together?"

He nodded. "Together. It's my graduation. No more tears, okay?"

Pike walked back in, holding her hand. Clair and 49 watched silently. Pike took Captain Jacobowski's seat and Jackie moved her chair tight against his.

Clair stayed quiet but slid Pike's beer over to him. He motioned a thank you, drinking a large gulp and placing it back down. He shifted his head toward his father. "I think Jackie and I will follow you back tomorrow and go see the police to get her cleared."

Clair's eyes shifted from Pike to Kris. "Hey, we don't start until Monday. I can tag along for support. We were going tomorrow anyway. I would like to meet your mother."

Jackie frowned. "Thank you, but that is not necessary."

Pike glanced over to Jackie, then back to Clair. "I'd like that."

Kris smiled. "That's settled. Your partner can ride up front with me while you two lovebirds sit in the back."

Jackie leaned forward. "We have our own car. I drove Pike's down here."

Pike forced a smile. "Great. It's been nearly a decade since we did a road trip, dad."

"Long overdue, son."

"We need to book a couple of hotel rooms. Mom doesn't have the room for all of us."

"We can show this little lady around the area you partially grew up in," Kris said, gesturing to Clair.

Jackie folded her arms in front of her chest and sat back. "There is nothing to see. The town is below average."

Clair corrected her. "I've never been. Well, once, but we won't talk about that."

Pike grinned and bumped her foot under the table. "Besides, I want to meet Kim."

Jackie huffed in displeasure. 49 observed her reaction, concerned about the situation. He didn't want this girl interfering with his plan. They ordered their food and 49 asked, "Where are you staying tonight?"

Clair answered for the group. "My condo."

Pike leaned in. "Do you have enough room?"

"We will figure it out."

Jackie smiled as though she had solved the problem. "We only take up one bed."

Pike cleared his throat, catching Clair's eyes. "We will figure it out."

Clair gripped her beer tightly, thankful it was thick glass, and drank.

Two's Company Four is a Crowd

THEY ALL HEADED OUT. 49 walked beside Kris and quietly asked, "When might I have a word in private?"

Kris eyed the threesome walking ahead of them. "You can join our delivery up North if you'd like."

49 watching Jackie flipping her hair as she latched onto Pike's arm. Wherever he was going, so was she. "Thanks, but I'll sit this one out. I suspect you already have a plan. I would only get in your way."

They stopped walking and casually faced each other. Kris glanced over at Jackie. "I'm hoping not to return with that one. She needs to go."

49 completely agreed, though he admitted, "Your kid was mighty upset when she went missing." He lowered his voice and continued, "You know, it could have been something else."

Kris held up his hand. "Don't go pushing your bullshit alien crap on me. I know what's in those trucks you drive. And the government is getting away with it. My boy just better be safe and not take the fall like Wade."

"Wade wasn't the saint you worshiped."

"You're right, Kittrick. He wasn't a saint. The man was a hero. A legend. Until the politicians saw their opportunity and got greedy."

"You still holding onto that conspiracy?"

Kris narrowed his eyes and pressed his index finger into 49's chest, "They killed him, Kittrick." 49 didn't flinch. Kris suddenly remembered the man's recent heart surgery and lowered his hand. "Just don't let my boy end up the same way for their bullshit, or you will start to really see people go missing."

49 stared hard at Kris. "Thirty-five-plus years, Hank. I've seen a lot that I can't explain myself. Wade got mixed up with the wrong crowd. Nothing to do with this branch. That was his own bad choices."

Kris's jaw tightened, though he didn't respond. 49 gave a slight nod. "Set a time aside for us to talk when you get back." He read every movement from Kris.

Kris narrowed his eyes. "I'll set time aside. Not sure what there is to talk about though."

49 faintly smiled. "Been a lot of years. We'll find something."

Kris gave an obligatory grin. "You never did finish that story about how you two met."

49 nodded. "Something for Pike to share on the drive. Say, those your wheels, Hank?"

Kris's lips twitched. "It's Kris. And yes."

"It's going to take me a bit to get used to that." They walked closer to the car. "She sure is pretty. Showroom quality. How much did that set you back?"

"Didn't even dent my pocket. Florida weather does its job keeping cars nice."

"You must spend a lot of time on that beauty."

He chuckled. "There's no need to measure time when you're doing something you enjoy."

"Suppose you're right . . . Kris." 49 grinned.

Pike called out to Clair, "We will meet you back there."

She nodded, hopping into her Jeep. Pike jogged over to 49, leaving Jackie standing at the side of his dad's Ford LTD. "You ready, dad? Are you coming to Clair's, Forty-Ni . . . Agent Kittrick?"

49 smiled proudly to Pike and gave him an affectionate squeeze of his shoulders. "You enjoy your company, kid. Congratulations, you did a fine job during the past month. I'll see you when you guys return."

Pike was disappointed. "Um, okay. You're not coming?"

"No. I've got paperwork to finish up."

"Sir? I'll call, all right?"

"Yes, always."

Pike mustered a grin through mixed emotions, though his heart raced anxiously. 49 had been there through everything this past month. He wanted him in Massachusetts to help deal with the hundreds of problems that could potentially happen. 49 always knew just what to do.

He could tell that his dad was unhappy with Jackie's presence. He would have Clair there with him, but he was already feeling the strain Jackie's arrival had created between them. This must have been how she had felt when Hanskon was around them. He didn't like it. Didn't need this trouble right now.

Feeling his heart flop, his throat tightened a little. He cleared it with a good "Ahem." He took a breath and reminded himself that he had 49 on speed dial. Clair would be there. Even though she would give him shit about Jackie, he knew where it would be coming from. Sometimes that's what partners do for each other.

He didn't make eye contact with 49 again, following his dad to the car with his father ordering, "Put the girl in the back. You sit up front with me. I don't know where your co-pilot lives."

Pike guided Jackie in the back seat. Clearly, she didn't like the arrangement, glaring up, eyes scrunched in disbelief that he actually left her back there all alone. He closed her door and moved to the front seat before turning to ask, "Where is my car, anyway?"

She scooted forward, touching his arm. "That nice officer at your work had me park it at the police station."

Pike smirked. "Nice officer? Didn't know we had one. Do you bring a bag?"

"Oh yes. It's in the car. I packed you a few outfits too. I wasn't sure what you have down here for clothing. You look very handsome in this.

Looks like you've been working out too." She glided her fingers along his forearm. "It's been too long."

He removed his arm beneath her touch. It had been a long time. He wasn't sure if he wanted to start back with her. Pike turned, facing forward and giving his dad directions to the base. He wanted to pick up his car and get Jackie to Clair's.

There sat his older-model Honda parked in front of the one-story building. Jackie handed him the keys, exiting from the back seat, not waiting for Pike to open the door. Pike questioned, "Maybe I should go clear this with the chief?"

She stood next to him. "Why? He just had me park this because I wasn't allowed on the base."

"Oh? Then I guess it's fine."

"They didn't think it was a good idea that I surprised you. They kept using code talk."

"Code talk?"

"I didn't understand what they were saying. I just figured it was some sort of military talk. They were nice to me though."

"Second thought, I better clear it that I'm taking the car."

Jackie shrugged. "Fine, I'll come in with you."

Pike signaled for his dad to wait, then headed into the building. The guy sitting in dispatch sat straighter upon spotting Jackie. She smiled. "See? I found him. Thanks for all your help."

He stood and walked over. "Nice. All set, Evans? It was a pleasure meeting your girlfriend."

Pike threw a quick glance to Jackie and grunted. "Hm. Thanks for your help. I'm going to take my car. Oh, do I need some sort of sticker for the gate?"

"You staying around here?"

Jackie lit up a flirtatious smile. "Hope so. People are so nice down here. Not like back home."

Pike remained straight-faced, "Not sure, but for now at least."

"We have base housing. You qualify."

Jackie touched his arm. "Would I be allowed to live with you?"

The dispatch guy answered for Pike with a sympathetic tone. "Sorry, miss. Unless you two are married, no civilian is allowed to live on base."

Pike quickly corrected him. "Not married or engaged. So that's a no."

"Guess you two will be looking off base. Not sure how your department works, but some of the guys get a housing allowance if they live off base."

She shrugged. "That's okay, hopefully things will change soon. You never know. But the allowance will certainly help us out while I get settled in down here." Jackie winked at him flirtatiously as a smile skimmed her mouthline.

Dispatch guy glanced from Pike to Jackie, ignoring what had happened. "Captain Jacobowski should have everything for you Monday."

Pike spoke before turning to leave. "Thanks man. I'm sure she's going to fill me in on opportunities. Come on, Jackie. Clair is waiting."

She waved to the dispatch guy. "Is he another one of your agent teammates?"

"Come on." He took her by the arm and moved her toward the door.

"What's the hurry?"

Pike let go outside and called out, "Follow me, dad."

Kris watched as the girl pointed back toward the door, complaining to Pike that he had been rude, before she climbed into the passenger seat.

Pike had expected one bag. Like, a simple bag to pack for a weekend trip. Jackie had filled four trash bags with her clothes, along with his duffle bag from the closet. They were all stuffed in the back seat. Pike shook his head in surprise and frustration before stuffing the key into the ignition.

"What did you bring?" He turned back, looking at the black lawn-and-leaf-size bags in his back seat. She grinned. "Don't worry. I have some of your stuff too."

Hard Truths

HE PULLED INTO CLAIR'S and parked next to her Jeep as Jackie hopped out and started carefully picking through the bags. He watched over her shoulder. He spotted his dress shirts and pants as she dug through. She had brought the clothes that she made him wear going out to clubs to meet their friends. There was none of his comfortable clothing, the simple stuff he liked to wear when he wasn't working.

Pike inhaled the scent of their laundry detergent. "You did laundry?"

She smiled over her shoulder. "I had plenty of time. I will make sure all our clothes are clean for now on. You were right to be mad. It won't happen ever again. I promise."

He observed all the stuff. She certainly took the time to pack. "All this cannot come in. Bring only what you need for the next sixteen hours. Everything else is staying in the car."

"Will it be safe?"

Pike looked around. "Really?"

Kris pulled in and parked next to Pike. His brown cowboy boot touched the pavement as he held the door for control. He stood, aviator sunglasses, white shirt, and straight-cut blue jeans. His looks belonged to that classic light blue LTD, posing like he should be lighting up a cigarette.

Kris took in the condo setup. He stopped searching as his eyes focused on Jackie rummage through the back seat stuffed with trash bags. Placing a toothpick in his mouth and stepping behind his car he motioned to Pike at the open trunk. He removed the toothpick from his clenched teeth, pointing to the bags. "She's staying?"

Pike's eyes darted to his father's as his dad raised the right corner of his mouth to challenge him to deny it, catching the toothpick with his back teeth. Pike frowned, slamming the trunk shut and demanding of Jackie, "Hurry up."

Pike could feel his frustration rising as he looked at the bags packed in his car. He wasn't even sure if they could park in these spots. He had gone a month without having his own transportation.

Pulling out his cell phone, he touched one button. Clair. "We're here. I'm parked next to you and my dad is on the other side of me. Are we good or do you want us to move?"

"Be right out."

The condo complex featured a row of tall, well-groomed shrubbery mixed with trees right down the center of the parking lot, giving the facing buildings that mirrored one another some privacy. Someone had thought this through, because it broke the parking lot up nicely.

Each condo's entry had two steps up with or without a covered porch. There was enough room to fit a couple of chairs to sit out and enjoy the community. The small porches were landscaped, with bushes and various blooming plants hanging or draped off the rails in yellow, orange, and red, making it feel like fall to the eyes but still summer on the skin.

Pike liked it here. Right here. In this very complex. Pike acknowledged green for the most part as he wondered how long it would stay warm down here. Green. The air felt clean as he took in a deep inhale. *Green*, his mind repeated. He felt a little rush of adrenaline.

Jackie's perfume hit him as she continued rummaging through the bags in the back seat. He could clearly smell it from all the way over here. Wow. Strong stuff.

He checked to see if anyone was staring at him. That was strange. What the hell was that rush from? It wasn't the perfume.

His toes tingled as he watched the ends of his boots. His mind thinking back to Massachusetts. Fall was quickly setting in up North, likely a good fifteen degrees cooler. *This is such a well maintained complex.*

Clair stepped out from her unit, walking a half circle to knock on the neighbor's door. An older woman held the door open as Clair pointed toward the cars and group. Pike waved at the neighbor with a friendly grin. She returned his smile and waved back, putting a supportive hand on Clair's upper arm, then waved again to the threesome before retreating back inside.

Clair strolled over, calling to Pike that they were all set where they were parked. Her mouth fell open at the sight of the bags of clothes Jackie was rummaging through. "Did she leave anything back in Massachusetts?"

Jackie heard that and popped her head out, looking over the car and narrowing her eyes to Clair. It was clearly not the response Clair had expected. *Especially since I'm housing this bitch for the night.* Jackie was already on probation for ruining Pike's graduation party. Clair reacted by squaring her stance. Pike might play the pussy in front of Jackie, but Clair was not putting up with it.

Pike joked. "Yes, my stuff."

Clair grew irritated at the thought of him defending her. "What?"

"You asked if she left anything back in Massachusetts? My stuff. Get it? It's a joke." Clair grinned, relieved her assumption was wrong.

Jackie challenged Pike. "I brought some of your things. Here, look." Pike closed the back door, holding Jackie's purse.

Clair laughed. "Doesn't go with your uniform."

He held it out, realizing he was holding a purse, and tossed it next to a bag Jackie was sifting through. She pulled out a couple of pairs of laced underwear, setting them on top of an outfit. All eyes focused on the frilly undergarments.

Pike had enough seen of this nonsense. Jackie could finish on her own. "Let's go in."

Kris, Clair, and Pike started to walk away as Jackie tried to halt them. "Wait! I'm almost done."

Clair answered for the group. "I'll leave the door open. Come in when you're finished."

Jackie scurried as she pulled out leggings and socks. That was all she needed for now. She called to Pike, "Honey, do you need me to bring in what I packed for you?"

He turned, walking backward. "All set, my stuff is already inside."

Jackie's mouth dropped open as she realized he had stayed here before. She rethought her outfits, digging through the piles again.

Clair poured the men iced tea while they all sat at the kitchen table. Pike asked if she wanted him to do anything, she shook her head. "Relax. You've had a busy afternoon." He smiled, grunting into his glass as he took a sip. Kris's eyes explored the room, observing all the framed certificates and achievements Clair had hanging in a cluster on the wall. He hmphed. "Marine."

Clair answered as if he had asked a question. "Yes sir." His eyes shifted from her to Pike. "Female Marine. You're screwed, boy."

Pike grinned, as did Clair. Pike answered, "She's already handed my ass back to me twice."

Clair laughed as Jackie walked through the door. "Pike?" She spotted them at the table. She observed the layout. "Nice place. Pike, we need a home like this. It would be perfect for us." She commented on the cluster of achievements, "Only I would put up a nice print instead of framed papers. Who wants to look at paperwork hanging on the wall?"

Clair sat back, picking up her iced tea as she answered Jackie. "I'll make note of that."

Pike muttered. "Sorry." His phone vibrated against the table, he turned it over. It was a message from Vonn Nash. "Nash."

Clair flicked her chin in his direction. "News?"

"Another missing person from that border town."

"The one we were stopped at?"

"Yup."

Clair balked. "Doesn't mean it's connected. Look, here she stands in the flesh. Right here in my home."

Jackie continued toward them, "I like to watch home decorating shows. My favorite one is on at ten every weekday. I have so many ideas about how I'm going to decorate our house. Maybe I should become a decorator. Is that a thing down here? I can't wait to get our own place. This is going to be so much fun, Pike. This is just the change we need."

Clair decided to have some fun with the situation. "Decorating shows? Ten at night? I'm usually in bed by then if I'm not on the road."

"No. We are usually asleep by then. Pike had to get up a four every morning. He wasn't exactly quiet about it, so I would wake up too."

"That's nice that you got up with him."

"I didn't get up. I tried it the first month but it just wrecked my day. I stay in bed and let him do his thing. I can usually fall back asleep after he leaves."

"Then watch television all morning?"

"I learn a lot from my shows."

"Do you work, Jackie?"

"Besides taking care of Pike? No. He takes up my time. I didn't realize how much I missed it until we split up for a bit. That really crushed me. From that day on I realized that he is my guy. He is the one."

Kris couldn't help himself. "Not only did you blow up my house, you leach off my boy. What did I tell you about women like this?" He waved off Pike, who was wide-eyed and about to say something.

Kris stood, holding Pike's shoulders down for him to stay seated. "It's the truth. Your mother was right. I wouldn't have believed it, but hearing this, seeing it for myself . . ."

"Dad. Please. Not the time."

Jackie's mouth dropped open. She turned her frame to the side and stood as tall as she could. She needed to say it because Pike wasn't, "Kim doesn't like me. She wants Pike to be under her thumb. Every time she calls she stresses us both out. I am so glad to be away from that woman. We couldn't do anything without her finding fault."

Clair kept on the subject of employment. "Realistically you should set your standards lower than holding out for a decorating job. Unless you have a degree?"

Jackie focused back on Pike, quickly raising up on her toes then back down. "I can find a job. Maybe a clothing store. I think I would like that. See all the latest trends first. That would be so much fun."

She looked around the place, checking to see if there were any doors down here besides the bathroom. "How many bedrooms has this place got?"

Clair smiled. "Two. Upstairs."

Jackie glanced to the stairs, holding her clothes in her arms. "Should I go put my things up there?"

Pike eyed Clair. "Maybe we should get a hotel room."

Clair waved him off. "Jackie can sleep in the spare room. You and your dad sleep down here."

Kris looked approvingly at the couch. "That's fine. Down here is perfect."

Jackie corrected Clair. "Pike will sleep with me. We are together."

Pike cleared his throat. "Jackie, you take the bed upstairs. I'll be fine down here with dad." He stood, not wanting her to publicly protest. Not her decision tonight with the sleeping arrangements. "Come on, I'll show you your room."

Jackie complained, muttering to him as they climbed the stairs. Kris glanced at Clair. "My opinion is set. I have a gut feeling about that one. I don't like her. Pike knows better, especially about that type. He has seen it himself when I fell into that trap. My fault. I've left him alone for too long."

Clair flexed her eyebrow. "I feel the same, but it's not up to us."

"Pike staying with you?"

"That was the plan until he figured out where he wants to be. I was going to let him crash here until he could save up enough for a down payment on something. But now that Miss MIA came out of hiding, he needs a new plan. She's not staying here after tonight."

Kris sipped his tea. "I'm working on a plan to leave her back in Massachusetts."

Clair agreed. "He can do so much better than her."

"As much as I don't like his employer, my kid is finally getting his shit together."

"She probably has ideas of getting pregnant."

Kris turned toward the stairs as Pike jogged down carrying his bag. "Don't get her pregnant, son."

Pike slowed his pace, wide-eyed, staring at them both sitting at the table. "Don't plan on it? I guess I know what you two are talking about."

Clair reminded him of their conversation not too long ago. "It's up to you, but as you can see from your car, she clearly has an agenda."

"I know. I'm not stupid."

"Just remember to pull out," lectured Kris.

Pike looked embarrassed. "Dad. Stop."

The three of them sat making plans for what time to leave in the morning. Clair and Pike searched for hotel availability. Clair wanted her own room, as did Kris. They booked three for tomorrow night.

Jackie made her way downstairs, changed into her leggings and midriff-length athletic sweatshirt. They all stared, acknowledging the effort she put into freshening up, then continued with their conversation. Jackie opened the refrigerator. Pike held his hand up as Clair whispered it was okay. Jackie bent over, looking at the water bottles, iced tea, and a few beers. "There is nothing in here that I drink. Do you have soda?"

"No. I don't touch the stuff."

"Pike, can we get some soda? I'm thirsty."

"Sonic is right around the corner." Clair pointed in the direction. "Short walk."

Jackie smiled. "I've always wanted to try them. I see their commercials. They look so good. Come on, honey, let's go. We can explore the area."

Clair gave him a way out. "It's just two blocks."

Jackie stepped away from the fridge. "Easy drive, then. I want to see the area. Let's look at houses."

Pike placed his hand on the table to stand up. Clair grimaced, her eyes narrowing. Pike was trying to avoid her look. He knew why she was giving it to him, but he just couldn't deal with this situation at this moment. Kris sat back, signaling to Pike. "I'm staying. Done enough driving for one day."

"I'll stay with your dad. I want to hear about the stuff he's not saying in front of you."

Kris rubbed his hands as a broad smile crept across his face. "Have I got stories for you."

Jackie waved Pike over, encouraging him to hurry. "Come on, honey. I'm thirsty."

He wanted to stay. "Here, take the car." Pike pulled out his keys.

She stomped her foot. "I don't know this area. Pike, come with me."

Pike smiled, thinking it might have worked. "Clair said it's just two blocks."

"I don't want to go alone. I don't know these neighborhoods."

Kris pointed out. "You made it down here from Massachusetts without your phone. Don't waste the gas. Two blocks will do your ass good to walk. Work off that shit you eat."

Jackie tilted her head, face pinched tight, staring from Kris to Pike. Now she was mad and showing it. "Pike!"

He maneuvered around the chair. "Be right back. Anyone want anything?"

Clair murmured up at him, "A set of balls."

He cupped her shoulder while passing behind her. "Still trying to coax mine out from the ice bath."

She smiled wide. "So that's where they went? I knew they were gone."

"Ha, ha, very funny. Be right back."

On the Eleventh Hour.

JACKIE SPENT ANOTHER hour outside at the car packing for the weekend back in Massachusetts. She finally returned inside. "I can't believe how warm it still is down here. This is going to be so nice. Did you know we have had the heat on since the end of August?"

Clair was helping Kris and Pike set up their beds for the night. Kris stood erect. "What?" He glanced over at Pike who was trying his best not to get sucked into this conversational mess. "You just like wasting my boy's money, don't you?"

Jackie's shoulders set back. "No, it's been cold there. Right, sweetie?"

Pike met Clair's eyes and he muttered sarcastically, "That's one way to describe it."

Clair grinned then, shifted her gaze to Jackie, whose smile had disappeared.

Pike adjusted the pillow on the recliner. "This will do for the night."

Clair tossed him an extra pillow. "More than I had last week."

Pike thought about Clair in the hotel chair pulled next to his bed. "Yes, it is."

Jackie witnessed the connection between them. "Pike should share the bed with me."

Everyone ignored her and, to her surprise, they were going to bed right now. Kris lifted the blanket and covered himself while adjusting the pillow even though it was still light out. "You're going to bed now?"

Pike reminded her. "We are leaving at three."

"In the morning?"

"That will put us arriving between 4 and 5 p.m. in Massachusetts. Hopefully more toward four than five."

"So, I have to go to bed now?"

"Or you can sleep in the car? Just be quiet so the rest of us can sleep."

"Can I have your phone?"

Pike eyed her. He wasn't giving up his phone. "No."

"I don't have one."

Clair interrupted. "You should have brought yours then. Pike isn't allowed to give his phone to anyone. He is a government agent now. It's policy. As a matter of fact, Evans, I need to store our firearms in my safe."

He nodded and handed his gun to Clair.

"Is there a TV in my room?"

"Sorry, no." She took Pike's gun. Now she was doubly armed. What an opportunity this was turning into. Clair enjoyed her thoughts.

"What am I supposed to do then?"

Kris answered, "Sleep."

"I guess I will go drive around by myself then."

Pike stood straight up. "You are not leaving. Go up to bed and stay there. We are all getting up early and there is no way you are leaving and then waking us all up in the middle of the night. Just go to bed, Jackie."

"I should just stay here while you guys go back."

Clair squashed her idea. "You're not staying here. I don't know you. Get a hotel room."

"I don't have the money. Pike, can you get me a hotel room?"

"I don't have extra money like that, Jackie. Buying food from Sonic is one thing. I have to pay for the hotel in Massachusetts."

"We get our own room, right? Alone?"

He nodded. "Yes."

"Okay, I will go."

Kris was trying to figure out how she had survived before meeting his son. "Where were you living before you moved into my house?"

"I had a place in housing. I gave it up when Pike asked me to move in."

"Might want to contact them when you get back."

"Why? I'm moving down here."

Clair's whole body twitched. Pike saw it. She chuckled, "That was weird? Must be tired. See y'all in the morning."

Jackie pointed out, "That's the first time I've heard you talk Southern."

Clair did not want to engage in further conversation and instead turned to climb the stairs. Pike ordered Jackie, "Go to bed. Two o'clock is going to come fast."

"Two? You said three."

"We are leaving at three."

"Do I get a kiss goodnight?" She swished, trying to entice him over.

Pike avoided her. "Let's just say goodnight."

"You're not even going to kiss me?" She stomped her foot.

"Goodnight, Jackie." Pike turned and settled in the chair. She audibly let out a rejected huff in protest and headed up the stairs louder than she normally walked.

Kris adjusted his pillow. "Think long and hard about that one, son."

Pike moved to find a position he could fall asleep in, thinking about how Clair had slept in his hotel chair for a week. Here he was in a comfy recliner having a hard time adjusting. "I am, dad. She is a little spoiled. I think I did that to her."

"You have been with this girl for how long?"

"Um, four months."

"You didn't do anything to her. That's her nature."

"I don't want to talk about it. Goodnight."

Bare footsteps plodded against the upstairs floor. Pike could recognize them anywhere. He knew the sound of her feet. Her gait when she walked. The way she dropped her right shoulder when mad. The Aussie shampoo scent in her hair.

The bathroom door closed. Pike lay there staring at the stairs. Clair was awake and getting ready.

Checking his phone, it read 1:30 a.m., time to get up. Pike heard the shower run while reaching over to the side of the recliner for the handle to collapse the footrest before climbing out of the chair. One big stretch toward the ceiling relaxed his body as he raked a hand through his hair. Their morning had begun.

The first order of business was to leave everything the way it had been before he and his dad turned the living room into a bedroom. Pike folded the blanket, placing it on the recliner quietly. The moonlight illuminated just enough of the downstairs for him not to crash into furniture as he made his way cleanly to the kitchen. Who was he kidding? He nearly had this place memorized.

Judging it was safe and far enough away from the couch to not disturb his dad, Pike risked flipping the light switch on in the kitchen. Yes, it was safe, he decided, as he leaned over the table checking to see how much light expanded the area.

Pike pulled the coffee maker away from the back wall of the counter. He hadn't considered the high-pitched squeaks the bottom made scraping across the counter. He stopped, picked up the coffee pot, and set it down quietly in front of him, plugging it in and filling the water-holding area.

Clair had one of those fancy single-cup machines that had you place a premeasured, sealed mini-cup into the top, press the lid down, crushing the seal, then stick your cup under.

Pike had never used one until he moved in. He pulled a mug down that resembled the one printed on the button. All five buttons displayed a tiny outline of different size cups with the ounce ratio. He propped it in place and waited.

The machine sputtered and spurted to life louder than he remembered as he darted around for something to quiet it. Too late. Kris was awake. He stretched, calling out a request, "Make one for me, Pike," then sat upright and stood, heading for the downstairs bathroom.

A chill shook Pike, like it was coming through the floor and straight into his feet. Wiggling his toes didn't help but the socks just might. He reached for his sweatshirt draped over a chair at the kitchen table, slipping it on. He then rubbed his hands together and walked over to his bag, pulling a pair of socks out.

With the first cup of coffee made, he prepared another for his dad. Fifteen minutes later Clair was ready, dressed, and walking down the stairs. She placed her bag near the door. "Smells like morning down here." She smiled, "Shower is available. I suggest you grab it now before we have to wake sleeping beauty. I can't imagine her being a few-minutes type of gal."

Pike chuckled. "Sleeping beauty? It's going to get ugly when we have to wake her."

"Not a morning person?"

"She's mean before ten o'clock."

Clair verbally jabbed at him, "When her television shows start?"

Pike made Clair a cup of coffee. "I see your sarcasm is fully awake."

She pulled out the stool at the counter. "I see she's pretty. But what were you thinking hooking up with that one?"

Kris walked toward them. "That is a legitimate question. I can see maybe for a few nights, but moving her in?"

Clair stood, moving away from the stool to retrieve the milk. Kris claimed the stool next to Clair as Pike slid their coffees in front of them. "She can be nice when she wants to."

"Pike, I'm not judging or trying to put you in a corner. Lord knows I have my skeletons. I just don't see what she is bringing to the relationship. No job. Clearly lives off the system. You can probably afford to pay for the both of you, but it's going to be tight. And from the looks of your back seat and trunk, that girl likes to spend money. Brand name money. What's going to be left for you?"

Kris shook his finger at Clair. "I like this gal. She makes a lot of sense. Listen to your partner, boy."

"Okay. Something to think about. I am going to go get ready, then wake up Jackie."

"I'll wake her up if you want. It is my house. That way she can't trap you into something you might regret."

Pike nodded. "Good idea. I'll be quick."

He was back down, showered, dressed, and bag in hand, placing it next to Clair's. She pushed up from her stool. "I'll go wake up the princess." She trotted up the stairs.

Pike announced, "I'll load our bags in the car."

"Okay," she answered. She thought of several different approaches on how to wake Jackie up. She grimaced, remembering the ways they woke her unit up in boot camp. Jackie wouldn't last a day in boot camp.

Clair raised her hand, making a tight fist, and banged loudly three times. She opened the door without an invitation, flipping the light switch on. Jackie sat straight up.

Clair ordered. "Get up, we're leaving in thirty minutes. The bathroom is free. Be ready. We have a schedule to keep. Thirty minutes."

Jackie gathered the hair out of her face, flipping it all back. "Where is Pike?"

"Loading the car. Get up. Now!"

Clair spun on her heels opening, the door wider, leaving the light on. Jackie threw off the covers, huffing out, "This is unbelievable." She slid out of bed, grabbing her bag, and purposely stomped to the bathroom, closing the door with force. Clair smiled from her own bedroom. She knew exactly the type of girl Jackie was.

She gave Jackie a minute to settle in the bathroom. This was the perfect moment. She walked out and knocked on the bathroom door, giving her countdown alerts. First was twenty minutes, next was fifteen, and the third was ten minutes, with Jackie complaining, "Would you quit that? I'll be out in a few minutes."

Clair grinned. "It's cold out this morning. You'll need a jacket. I hope you packed one."

"Leave me the fuck alone."

Clair turned up her alligator smile knowing she was hitting on Jackie's nerves.

Pike grabbed a few waters from the fridge, anxious to get going. Clair was about to run back up for Jackie's five-minute warning before he stopped her on the first step. "I'll get her."

Kris stood. "I'll bring the car out front."

Pike was about to climb the stairs, but turned abruptly, "No, dad. We will go to you, just in case Jackie needs something else from my car."

"That's just giving her power to run the show," protested Clair.

"We are ahead of schedule. She might need a coat."

Clair reached out to Pike. "Give me those. I'll take care of that."

He handed the water bottles over. "Be right back. And thank you. For everything." He flashed a smile and turned to jog up the stairs. He knocked on the door. "Jackie, come on. Let's go."

He heard the knob unlock as the door opened, pushing back the towels that had been left on the floor. She quickly glanced over his shoulder, looking around behind him. Her hair was up in another towel. "I haven't even dried my hair yet. I still have to do my makeup. That girl keeps coming up here and pressuring me. Give me thirty minutes and I will be done, I promise."

Pike walked in, picked all her belonging up off the sink, and dropped them in her bag.

"What are you doing?"

"We are leaving. Now."

"What? Wait!"

Clair appeared in the doorframe. "We are leaving right now. You had plenty of time."

"My hair is wet!"

"It will be dried by the time we cross over to Virginia. You can bring the towel."

Pike zipped her bag and stood up from his crouched position. Jackie had used Clair's shampoo. He could smell it on her, and that irritated him. He picked up Jackie's bag and secured it over his shoulder, then placed his hand on her backside, moving her. "Come on."

She looked around the bathroom wildly to make sure he had grabbed everything as he nudged her forward.

"Are you kidding me?!" She tried to resist being moved.

Clair stepped aside, with Jackie still complaining. "First you wake me in the middle of the night and now I can't even get ready."

Clair offered sweetly, "You can sleep in the car, then when you wake up continue your production line. Your hair will be dried by then too. Win-win, right?"

Jackie narrowed her eyes as they blazed murderously into Clair. Clair physically pulled the towel from her hair. "On second thought, the towel stays."

She tossed it onto the bathroom floor with the other three. Jackie, still holding her hair from Clair's swift towel pull, turned to Pike. "Let's take our car. I don't want to ride with them."

"Come on, Jackie, everything is already planned."

"Then I am staying."

"Where, Jackie? Where are you staying?"

Clair corrected her. "We could leave her at the police station. They could make arrangements to transport her to Massachusetts separately. I bet the insurance company will pay for that."

Jackie clenched her jaw, staring from Clair to Pike, and stomped down the stairs. Pike shook his head. "That was a little harsh."

Clair shrugged. "Got her to move and I don't have to buy another towel now." There was a smug glint in her eyes. "Win-win, Evans."

Pike found Jackie's coat after moving a few piles of clothes. He handed it to her and she slipped it on before climbing into the back seat of the LTD. She folded her arms and pressed herself as far away from Pike as she could get, staring out the window and wishing she had never made the trip down here. By the time they reached Virginia she was asleep, easing the tension inside the car.

Pike knew this side of Jackie, so he felt he needed to explain. Clair turned to face him, whispering her irritation over Jackie's spoiled attitude. "Don't you dare make excuses for her. She is rude. If I ever acted like that in front of company my mother would have made sure . . ." Clair stopped.

Pike asked, "What? Spank you?"

Clair looked away and cleared her throat. She inhaled as if trying to keep something buried. It took only a moment to regain her composure, then she made eye contact with Pike again. Pike saw the dark shadow in her eyes. It changed to irritability again. "Point is she knew our schedule yet thought it was okay to stray from the plan. Your girlfriend is a self-centered jerk."

Pike glanced over to Jackie. Clair added, "She left Saturday? And she shows up Wednesday afternoon? Where has she been for four days? Maybe she was ready to move out of your dad's house and she shacked up with another guy, only he realized he didn't want her so she made her way down to you."

Pike's heart plummeted down hard in his chest. Kris turned to Clair. "Damn, woman. I would not want to be the man who crossed you. Are you a detective or something?"

"No. But there was a guy who crossed me. Fool me once . . . . Right?"

There was a buzzing in Pike's head. Everything Clair said could have been true. Pike pulled out his phone and checked her social media. Still nothing posted since Saturday. He started to poke around her friends' status. Tammy's most recent post said no one had heard from Jackie since Saturday. He scrolled through the comments, reading each one.

Kris and Clair continued their conversation from the front seat. Clair chuckled about something and turned to see Pike staring at his phone. "Did you find something?"

Pike's eyes flicked up. His whole manner, the way he jerked his head up so quickly, suggested he had been caught doing something he wasn't supposed to. His face flushed.

She softened. "I'm sorry. Sometimes it sucks being right." He flipped his phone over and placed it on the seat. He observed Jackie sleeping against the door. She hadn't smoked once since she arrived. Did she quit? Did she borrow money to drive down to North Carolina? Was she in a relationship with some other guy while she was also with him? Did she only come back to him after someone else kicked her out?

His hands started to sweat. It was getting warm in the car. His nerves buzzed. Buzzing like when he was jolted twenty years ago when he grabbed onto his uncle Wade's electric fence.

He removed his sweatshirt. Clair turned to watch him and reached down over the back of her seat to place a hand on his knee. "I can only imagine what is going through your head. Now is not the time to confront her. Do it in your hotel room. Alone."

Pike nodded softly, watching the hand she had offered to comfort him, and answered, "Okay."

They stopped in Baltimore to take a break and eat. Kris had a favorite diner just off the highway that had become a regular stop during his many years on the road. The parking lot had plenty of room to park several tractor trailers.

Pike shook Jackie awake by her shoulder. He didn't intend to be heavy-handed but she awoke startled. She opened her eyes and sat straight up. "Where are we? What time is it?" She stretched a bit upon realizing they were still in the car.

"Baltimore. It's just past nine. There's a diner. We're going to go in and get something to eat."

She ran her fingers through her hair, trying to comb it out some. It was dry with a lively wave. She hated this look. Pike admired it. He only saw her like this on the weekends right after she woke up, and then only until she made her way to the bathroom where she would brush it straighter or put it up in a loop bun on the top of her head. "Come on," he encouraged her, "I'm hungry."

Jackie's eyes swept the back seat, spotting her handbag on the floor near her feet. Her hair fell forward. She tucked some strands behind her ear, plunking the purse on her lap and digging for her compact mirror and lip gloss. She angled the mirror around, checking her face and hair, sighing heavy in disgust over how she looked. She dabbed some gloss on for a subtle improvement. No makeup and her hair in waves. At least no one knew her around here.

Pike shut his door, stretching out from the long drive. Clair took a look around the neighborhood while Jackie asked if this part of town had gangs as she stared at the rows of brick buildings mirroring both sides of the street.

They all started walking toward the diner. An awning displayed a smiling cartoon coffee mug splashing its liquid, marching in front of a matching cartoon-themed plate with utensils following.

Kris opened the diner door for everyone to enter. Clair led the way inside. A middle-aged waitress in designer jeans, a red plaid untucked linen shirt, and a black tank top revealing her cleavage greeted them a hearty good morning, while spreading her arm out, inviting them to pick their seating.

Clair chose a table off to the side but remained standing and asked Pike to order her a coffee. She turned without saying another word and walked toward the restrooms.

The waitress pulled a few placemats out from the side cubby and grabbed four sets of napkin-wrapped utensil. She handed out the menus and took everyone's drink orders.

Jackie asked for soda. Pike ordered orange juice and Clair's coffee. He knew just how she liked it, asking for milk on the side. Jackie asked Pike why he was ordering for Clair. He shook his head, brushing it off. Kris requested a tall glass of sweet tea and winked at the waitress. She smiled back, acknowledging his compliment.

"Dad, that's all I've seen you drink besides the one coffee this morning. When did that happen?"

Kris adjusted his head to look over the menu. It had been a while since they last spent time together. "I always drank this stuff. You just aren't around enough to notice."

Pike recognized the jab. "I meant to come down. Work and looking for work just kept getting in the way."

"I can't understand you settling for those low-wage jobs. You should have been out on the road as soon as you got out. I gave you names. They were looking for drivers. Now you've gone and wasted three years. That's a lot of years, son, in this industry."

"I don't see it as a waste. Look at my new job. I wouldn't have gotten this if I had gone right out on the road for the private sector."

"We will see if it's a blessing or a curse. Wade is turning over in his grave, I just know it."

Pike looked away. He knew what his dad was getting at.

Clair returned and it was Jackie's turn to leave the table, eyeballing Clair as she walked past. Kris addressed Pike and Clair, "Once we finish eating I will step outside and call the insurance company. Find out what they want to do about the girl."

Clair nodded. "If they want a full investigation it could take days. We have to be back by Sunday night. We start work."

"What if they need Jackie to stay, dad? Then what?"

The way Clair asked her next question made it clear she was ready for an argument. "Is she coming back with us?"

The waitress carried over a tray of drinks and took their food orders. Pike ordered for Jackie. He knew how much of a picky eater she was when they ate out. She would eat pancakes though. The waitress left. Pike answered, "I don't know? I can't dump her there and go."

Clair leaned forward, jabbing her index finger into the table. "Yes. Yes, you can. She's what, twenty-six?"

"Twenty-five."

Clair cleared her throat. "She is on government assistance, right?"

"She gets food money."

"Rent money?"

Pike slouched. "I don't know. She lived in block housing when I met her."

"Alone?"

"Yes. The place was a dump."

"Then she gets rent money."

"She does?"

"What's the cost of living in Massachusetts?"

"I don't know."

"Average apartment? How much is rent?"

"About seven hundred and up."

"They probably give her eight hundred easily."

Pike's head buzzed. Was she getting money for housing? He thought it was just food allowance on her card.

Jackie returned with eyeliner and lipstick on. "Much better."

Pike turned to her. "I ordered you pancakes."

She smiled. "You always know what I like. Thank you."

"Your EBT card. Do you get money for housing on that?"

Jackie seemed slightly embarrassed as she looked from Clair to Kris before answering quietly, "Yes. Why?"

"How much?"

She settled her hand on his knee, whispering, "Can we talk about this when we are alone?"

He growled out, "How much?!"

"This isn't the time or place for this."

"How much?"

She removed her hand quickly from his leg. "Nine hundred."

"Nine hundred? A month?"

"Yes? Why?"

"To spend toward rent and stuff?"

"Pike, why are you asking?"

"Answer the damn question."

"Yes."

He threw his napkin down. "And you couldn't buy a damn box of detergent so I could have a clean uniform?" He stood up as the confused look on her face followed him leaving. "But you said I just needed to buy the food?"

She turned to Clair then Kris. She started to get up. Kris held out his hand for her to stop. "Let him be. He will come back. I think you'd better start wrapping your head around the idea that you will not be returning with us."

She started to cry. "But all my stuff is in North Carolina."

Clair offered, "We will ship it to you."

"I don't have anywhere to live?"

"I'm sure there is emergency housing for people in your situation."

"I don't want to go back. This was the one chance to get away from . . ."

The waitress came back over with their food, glancing from Jackie to Clair to Kris. Kris stood. "I'll go get him."

Clair offered, "I can text him."

"Text. All you young are people on your phones for everything. You're replacing human connection."

Kris walked away as Jackie pushed her plate to the side. Clair dug right into her breakfast burrito. "Don't waste food."

"I'm not hungry."

"Then don't waste money. Especially Pike's."

Jackie pulled her plate back in front of her, turning to see Pike and Kris walking back in. Pike sat down forcefully. He started eating right away.

Jackie angled her head toward him, mustering a weak, "I'm sorry."

He answered with a mouth full of eggs, "I don't want to hear it. I don't want to talk about it."

She nodded. There was no way she wanted to talk either, especially in front of the other two. Jackie followed Clair from the corner of her eye. Was she interfering with her and Pike getting back together? Playing with her food, she finally took a small bite of her pancakes.

Pike and Clair swapped seating in the LTD. Five hours of minimal conversation made the last leg of the journey seem to take forever. Clair stared at the back of Pike's head, telepathically willing him not to bring Jackie back.

Kris pulled right into the Agawam Police Department parking lot, explaining gently to Jackie that she would need to talk to the detective.

Kris walked her in while Pike held his ground and remained in the car. He started to crack as she turned from the entrance to look at him sitting there. She turned back and walked in willingly, with Kris holding the door.

Pike exhaled. "Shit. I should go in."

Clair reached forward. "If you do, it will send the wrong message. You've stood firm for the past six hours."

"Fuck!" He shouted out, clenching his fingers in a fist. "She didn't blow up the house."

"Leave that for the cops to figure out."

"Who would walk willingly into the station if they were guilty?"

"Pike, why are you torturing yourself like this? Twenty-four hours ago you were happy. You had a smile on your face. Everything was perfect. From the minute you saw her you have been uptight, cranky, protective, and stressed out."

"I don't know. Jackie doesn't have anything. She can change."

Clair unbuckled and scooched forward. "Says everyone. Including me. They don't change. Dude, she has more than you think. Besides, she's clearly resourceful. If you give in, you will always be wondering about her. Who is she with? What is she doing? Where is she going? I know from experience. Believe me, it's crippling."

Pike turned his head. Clair's eyes softened. "I like you better when you're happy. You're almost tolerable."

"I can't believe she just left piles of our dirty clothes. My clothes. And couldn't buy a box of detergent."

Clair sat back. "That is pretty bad. Just goes to show you she is not a team player. The best thing you could do for yourself is let her go. See if she can change on her own. If she straightens out maybe there will be a future with her."

"I like that. Give her room to grow up."

"Now you're thinking like a big boy."

Pike condescendingly grinned at Clair, who was enjoying being a wise-ass. "Okay, I'll go with that."

"You can share my hotel room if you want to give her a room of her own."

"Oh shit, that's right. Do you think the cops will keep her overnight?"

Clair stared out the window. "No. A few hours, I imagine. We can check in. Have her call. I'm assuming your dad will be willing to come pick her up and bring her back?"

"I bet he's working that out with the cops right now."

Kris returned a half hour later. "Let's check into the rooms."

Pike inquired, "Are they going to call you when they're done?"

"Why?"

"What about Jackie?"

"What about her? Let the state take care of that trainwreck."

"Dad, we can't just dump her here."

"Now look, son. I've never seen you so miserable. We've got to meet your mother in three hours. I want to drive over and look at the house. The insurance is going to find temporary housing since she was listed at the address. If they find foul play she's going to jail."

"Dad!"

"Calm down, boy. I have the number to the woman who is taking charge of your little friend. She will be looked after. I don't think she is getting a car, since she didn't own one."

Kris started the LTD. "Kojak said if she had a state phone they will replace it for free. She has three hundred on her. I overheard her telling someone. She's set for now." He made Pike bring in her suitcase and watched him looking back at the door as he walked to the car.

Kris backed up and pulled away with Pike's eyes fixed on the front entrance until it disappeared out of sight. His stomach formed a knot and he wondered what might be happening to Jackie right now.

Memory Lane

PIKE INSISTED ON HIS own room for the night. He wanted to make sure if the insurance company didn't come through that Jackie would at least have someplace to stay.

Clair happily claimed the back seat all to herself. Pike played tour guide, pointing out some of the places the area was known for, like the amusement park and the state fair held in the next town over along with the Basketball Hall of Fame. He glanced over at his dad.

"Can I borrow the car tomorrow? There are a few places I want to bring Clair to while we are up here."

"I have appointments tomorrow. Maybe your mother can let you borrow her car."

"Okay. Doubt it, but I'll ask."

They arrived in front of where the house used to be. Kris stared at the fencing they installed to secure the grounds. "Holy . . ."

Pike and Clair stepped out of the car. Pike zipped his jacket and looked up to see the V formation of the geese traveling south, heard the honking sounds as they flew overhead.

Kris looked for anything familiar. "The whole damn house is gone."

"Yes."

"You said there were two containers?"

"Yeah. I drove one and Clair drove the other."

"Any word?"

"They don't tell us anything."

"Can you find out if the girl blew it up?"

"Let me call 49."

"Who's 49?"

Pike flushed, "I mean Agent Kittrick." Clair smirked.

Pike walked away, now on the phone with 49.

Kris stepped along the fencing line. "I've seen tornados wipe houses clean off their slabs. Nothing like this though. I imagine this is what a bomb going off would look like. Just a big whole in the earth. Your boys did a good job cleaning it up."

Pike walked back, following his dad. "He's going to try to find out something."

"Take some pictures of this, boy. Words can't describe this act of injustice."

Kris rocked his body with each step as he explored the fencing, looking for anything familiar. The yard was groomed cleaner than they ever kept it. His tilted his head upward, following the trees and squinting at the angle of the sun. Fresh branches had broken off, bearing charred marks indicating a blast of fire.

The two houses nearby also showed damage where debris had hit their sides. One of the neighbors walked out.

"Is that you, Pike?"

Mrs. Johnson was relieved to see him. "Your mother said you moved to North Carolina? I figured that's where your girl was heading to. She loaded up your car all morning on Saturday despite the rain. Even had some boys come by to help move a few of the bigger furniture pieces."

"Furniture? Like what?"

"Looked like the bedroom set on the first load. Then the kitchen set, lamps and a few boxes the next loads."

Pike darted forward angrily. "How many loads did you see?"

"Three maybe? You look surprised. Oh dear, did I put my foot in my mouth?"

He turned toward his dad. "No."

Kris narrowed his brows at Pike. "Where did my stuff go?"

Mrs. Johnson grew worried. "I should have called your mother. She said Jackie was moving out. I assumed it was her stuff."

Pike gritted his teeth. "She didn't have anything."

Clair stepped forward. "It's either in storage or she sold it."

Pike glanced down, pulling his ringing phone from his pocket. It was 49. He stepped away from the group.

Kris asked, "Did you tell anyone about the furniture?"

"The adjustor came out this morning to check my house, but I didn't say anything about her. I did tell them your house clearly got hit by lightning. The flash and explosion had me running. I am shocked my windows didn't shatter."

"So, it did get struck by lightning?"

"The flash lit up the entire block. Sounded like a bomb went off. Honestly, I thought it was my house that was struck at first. I looked outside when I thought it was safe and your house was gone. Gone. Nothing left. Had me shaking for a good hour. I don't know how I managed to call the police. I could barely speak."

Clair stepped forward. "Pike needs to know all this."

She jogged over to where Pike was talking to 49. "Hey, is that Kittrick?"

He nodded.

"Put him on speaker."

Pike warned 49 he was switching to speaker and Clair was with him. "Get this, can you hear me, Kittrick?"

"I can hear you."

"Pike's neighbor is here, and she says the house got struck by lightning. It blew up. She saw the flash and had to duck for cover. She thought it was her house that got hit. When she looked outside at Pike's the house was gone."

Pike grew wide-eyed, his brain zapped, and a lump suddenly formed in his throat while a knot tugged in his stomach. His body buzzed. Heating up, he handed Clair his phone while he unzipped his jacket.

She watched, "You, okay?'

"Hot. I'm fine," he said while unzipping his inner-layer sweatshirt as well to cool down his core.

She continued. "His house is confirmed to have been stuck by lighting. Could lighting have done that? Or could Jackie have left the stove on and would the combination of propane building up and lightning make the house blow to bits?"

49 paused. "All very interesting theories. Can I share this with Maggie?"

Pike took back his phone. "Of course."

"I will call you when I have more to report on the remnants."

"We will too. Thanks. I wish you'd come with us."

"No. It's better I'm here. When are you heading back?"

Pike shrugged to Clair. She shrugged back. He guessed. "Saturday? Dad has to talk with the insurance company tomorrow. I was going to take Clair around, but maybe we better go with Dad. Find out what they know." Clair nodded, agreeing.

"Okay, kid, call with any updates."

"Will do." Pike pressed down on the screen, ending the call. "I have to get in touch with Jackie. Find out what she did with my furniture."

"I'm sure your dad knows how to contact her."

They walked back to Kris and Mrs. Johnson.

"I can tell you one thing. I am so happy no one was in the house." Her eyes were overflowing with tears as she reached for Pike's arm. "Thank the lord you both left."

Pike's head shifted, glancing to the hole in the ground. His chest tightened and he massaged at a nonexistent knot in the center of it, remembering what it felt like when he thought Jackie was in the house. "Me too, Mrs. Johnson."

Pike's mother, unwilling to wait any longer for them to get out of the car, walked out of the house to greet them in the driveway. She studied Clair as she walked toward them. Taller than she expected. A lot tougher-looking as well. This girl was no Barbie doll like Jackie. Still, she wasn't sure she liked this type of girl for Pike either.

Kim headed straight for Pike, hugging him then pushing him back an arm's length as she physically checked him over, bending her upper body to each side.

"My goodness. You have filled out. Do they have you on that muscle-building crap? Make you drink those *workout* shakes?"

Pike cocked an eyebrow. "No, nothing like that. Mom, this is Agent Morris, my partner."

Kim lifted an eyebrow at the word partner as she let go of Pike, studying Clair's expression. "So, you're his new partner?" Kim leaned in, giving Clair the benefit of the doubt. "Keep him in line."

Clair flashed her a knowing smile. "Oh, I plan on it."

Pike chuckled. "I can't get away with anything, mom."

Kim nodded. "Good. That's just what you need."

Pike covered his hands over his heart. "Ouch."

Kim ignored him. "You can call me Kim. I'm glad to see you are older. I have had enough of those young airheaded girls."

Clair's eyebrows shot straight up as her mouth slightly opened. Kim continued looking over Pike. "He needs to be around mature, serious influences. He's not a leader. Pike is a follower. The women he's picked these last few years would lead him right into the fire if it wasn't for me stopping him."

Pike stepped into her. "Enough, mom. I'm starving. What's to eat?"

"Meatloaf. Mike is inside waiting. Show your partner in. Kris, I need to talk to you."

Pike flicked his head in the direction of the walkway. As Clair stepped away from Kim, she curled her lip and flipped her palms up at

Pike. He just waved her to come along and whispered as she closed in, "It's going to get worse. Bet my mom's worse than yours."

Clair nodded. "Doubt it, but might be close."

In the drive, Kris stood his ground, waiting for the complaints.

Pike walked Clair in and introduced her to Mike. She snickered, "Mike and Pike."

Pike frowned. "Don't start."

Dinner opened with Kim voicing her dislike of Jackie. All her dislikes, actually. No one said a word about the furniture leaving the house. Kim would have lost it. Food was shoveled into mouths as Kim ranted and pointed out to Pike every so often how incompetent he was with picking women in his life.

Pike began feeling a headache coming on and tried to stop his mother. "Enough about Jackie. I am sick of hearing you go on and on. No more talk about her. Understood?"

Kim was surprised Pike had raised his voice to her. She held her fork hovering over her plate. Her eyes darted to Clair, accusing more than asking, "Where are you from?"

Clair gave a little more detail about being in a military family and everywhere they had lived over in Europe. Clair could speak three languages, which rendered her a cultured and curious woman who fascinated Kim. Mike was still stuck on her being a Marine. Kim's eyes darted to Mike then Kris. "I wanted to travel. I should have been a flight attendant. Fly all over the world."

Kris set down his fork. "You did travel. All over the United States."

She set down her utensils and picked up her wine, grumbling at him. "Not how I wanted to travel. I don't know how people find that enjoyable."

Kris sat back. "I don't know why you would travel any other way."

Her eyes narrowed at Kris.

Clair interrupted by sharing one of her missions while Kim looked on in horror that she had had to sit in a swamp for hours waiting on orders.

Kris watched Clair as she spoke, then thanked her for her service when she was done speaking. She nodded politely, admitting that there were times when she still missed it.

Kim proudly added that Pike served in the Army. Pike held his hand up, saying, "Don't even go there," making Clair chuckle.

Two hours filled with embarring stories of Pike growing up was all he could take. Clair recognized the stress in him from the way his shoulders were tense and he kept looking down at the carpet. She patted his knee, announcing it had been a long day. It was time for them to get back. Never had Clair heard a mother beat down her own son like that. Maybe Jackie had a valid point.

Pike announced they were leaving while Kris expelled a welcoming sigh, standing up before anyone could dispute it. He wanted out of his ex-wife's house now.

Clair shook Mike's hand and thanked Kim while Pike nudged her toward the door. In the car, he kept glancing down at his phone. No messages, no calls. Kris joked about how he used to be trapped with Kim in the tractor and for years she had worn him down. Buying that house in Agawam turned out to be the best decision he had ever made.

It was a no-brainer. They were all going to the insurance assessment tomorrow.

The Price is Right

THREE SEPARATE ROOMS for three separate people. Morning arrived. Five o'clock to be exact. It was too early to wake up his dad, so Pike woke up Clair instead.

She opened the door at the sound of his knock, mostly dressed but her hair was still wet. He had seen her stripped down to her bra and panties before. The black tank top, cargo pants, and wet hair felt arousing. He needed a distraction. Fast. He focused on Jackie's whereabouts.

He hadn't heard from her. and Kris would be the only person to know how to find out her whereabouts. One call to the insurance company and he had her new phone number and the name of the hotel where she was staying.

It was only nine in the morning, but Pike tried calling anyway, hoping she was awake. Pike touched the numbers on his phone. One ring. "Hello."

Her answer drew a sigh of relief from Pike. "Jackie, I need to talk to you about something."

"Me too, Pike. Can you come over? I don't have a car."

Kris, Clair, and Pike packed up and headed into downtown Springfield. They arrived just after ten. Clair pulled her phone out of her pocket checking the time, "Bet she's watching her decorating show. Are you sure she will want to be interrupted?"

Pike lifted an eyebrow. "Very funny. Come on."

They entered the lobby. Clair and Pike wore standard work attire and Kris was in his cowboy boots, jeans, button-down business shirt, and brown leather jacket. He looked like he had just come off the ranch ready to make a deal. This hotel was a significant upgrade over where the three of them were currently staying.

He double-checked the number displayed on the little gold plaque outside her door, making sure it matched the piece of paper in his hand, and knocked. Jackie opened the door disappointed that Clair and Kris stood waiting behind Pike. "I don't want them in here. I feel threatened. They don't like me."

Pike looked over his shoulder. "Them?"

She held the doorknob keeping the door close to her. "Yes. Just you Pike. They can go wait in the car."

Kris exchanged frustrated glances with Clair regarding this new game Jackie was playing. Clair had no intention of letting the troublemaker have the upper hand. "I'll go, but Kris needs to hear what you have to say in regard to the house and its content. Especially its contents. *His* belongings . . . and what happened to them and where they moved to?" She flexed her left eyebrow and quickly returned to her poker face.

Jackie refused. "No. You both go. Get out of here. I am only talking to Pike."

He turned, holding his hands up to stop what they were going to say and reassuring Clair it would be fine.

Clair leaned in, eyeing Jackie from around Pike's shoulder, "We'll wait in the lobby."

Pike nodded to her answer. "Okay." He back toward Jackie, who held the door open a little wider, inviting him in.

Clair quickly scanned the inside of the massive room. Her eyes landed on the television with what looked like a decorating show on. She shook her head, as Jackie displayed a triumphant gaze and shut the door hard on them.

Clair twisted her lips. "Bitch."

Kris signaled with his index finger. "Don't trust or like that one. Pike isn't thinking with the right head."

Inside the room, Pike tilted his head to the side. "Was that necessary?"

Jackie shrugged a shoulder. "Yes." This was her hotel suite and she did not have to be polite anymore. This was her domain and she was calling the shots from here on. Pike stepped deeper into the room, immediately spotting several bags of new clothes draped over the chairs. "Go shopping?"

"Yes. The insurance company says the house was struck by lightning. I am cleared."

"That's what my neighbor said."

"The insurance lady had me fill out a list of what was mine in the house."

"You didn't have anything? Just the clothes that are all down in North Carolina."

She hesitated, stopped what she was going to say, and let the pause linger. Her eyes met his and she softly added, "I didn't mention any of that." She watched for his next reaction. He could ruin it all for her.

"What did you say to them?"

"They gave me a check for $10,000."

"Jackie. What did you tell them?!"

"They are paying for this suite for three months and I can order anything off the menu up to $60 a day."

"Jackie. Why did they give you a check for that amount?"

"We could put that money toward our own place. I'm sure you will get money as well. There's our down payment. We will be able to get our very own place, just like I always wanted. Something nice. I will get a job, I promise. We can do this, Pike. Together."

"Jackie, you didn't have anything in there but clothes. Which reminds me. What furniture did you remove from my dad's house?"

"Our bedroom furniture, the kitchen set, and some living room stuff."

"That's my father's stuff. You had no right to take any of that. Where is it?"

"Don't worry. It's all safe. I have it in storage. But we probably should get rid of it now that we can afford to buy new stuff. Something we can pick out together."

"You stole all that!"

"I took it so we could have something to start out with."

"Jackie. You stole."

"No. I still have it. It's just in a different location. And you know about it now."

"You never said one word about moving any of that."

"I was too excited to finally see you. I was going to tell you, then your dad accused me of blowing up the place, and your teammate . . . she is just awful."

"Jackie. You'd better give the insurance company back their check."

"Why?"

"You could go to jail."

"No. It's my money."

"Jackie, my dad knows about the furniture you took. There is an eyewitness. If you don't, he's going to tell the insurance company."

"Why does your dad hate me?"

"Did you leave the stove on?"

She turned away. "I'm not giving the money back."

"Answer my question. Did you?"

"If we are not going to be together then I need this money to replace what I gave up moving in with you."

Pike's heart pounded in his chest. A high pitch sounded in his ears. He watched every facial muscle twitch on her as she turned back, trying to cover up her expression. Jackie couldn't look him in the eyes. He knew the answer. His dad was right. "I can't do this. I can't lie like you do. I am a government agent now. I can't be tied to a person like you."

"Pike!" Wide-eyed and desperate, she realized he was cutting her loose.

"No, Jackie. You do whatever you want with that money. But I am going to tell the truth. They will have you on insurance fraud."

He turned for the door. Jackie pleaded, "Pike, don't go!"

"Don't bother returning to North Carolina. I am sure the insurance company will want your clothes."

"Pike. Wait. Please!"

He jerked his hand out from her desperate grip, easily breaking the connection as she scrambled to reach for him again. Pike pushed her off as he made his way toward the door. Jackie jolted, flying backward and hitting the floor hard as she screamed out from the shock and pain.

He froze, confused. His face began to heat up. His eyes stared first at his arm and then Jackie. He mentally marked the distance, how far back she landed away from him. It was only a slight push but there she was, sprawled on the ground a good ten feet away, both her hands flat on the floor in front of her completely, stunned and unable to move.

Her eyes filled with tears, bottom lip quivering as she rocked forward and moved her legs to the side to stand. He held her gaze only a moment, shifting to observe his hand again. It was a only tiny push to get her away from him.

Was this a trap? Did she overreact to the push, just playing this out like he threw her down? He didn't want any part of what she might be doing and the lengths she was going to in order to achieve it.

There was no way he used that amount of force. His body hummed. He felt jitters throughout. He glanced down as if something would be visible to explain the subtle vibration. Nothing. He opened and closed his right hand, making sure he still had control over it.

He looked back at Jackie once more and she really started crying. "You hurt me. Physically hurt me, Pike."

No answer was the correct answer. She was probably going to call the police.

He opened the door, walked through and then slammed it shut. His eyes widened as the frame shoot and the aftershock sounds vibrated throughout the wall.

Pike released the knob. He realized that he felt unusually hot, and began tugging at his shirt collar. He stepped back, watching the whole frame of the door, expecting it to do something all on its own as he stepped away again. The sound it made on closing was too loud. His eyes darted from door to door in the hallway. Adrenalin pumped through him. He needed to leave. Get out of there before people came out of their rooms to see what was going on. He didn't want to be seen leaving, he needed to get away from the scene.

Pike walked quickly, his head buzzing with the replay of Jackie sprawled out on the floor and the door nearly coming off the hinges. He tried to make sense out of the guilt he was feeling.

The stairs were across from the elevators. He had to keep moving. The door felt light for being metal and he used more force than he should have, causin it to hit the wall with a crack. His heart pounded in his ears and he grabbed the handrail, moving his feet as fast as they could go. What was happening?

He descended, practically running down the stairs. Then he jumped a whole flight. His feet hit perfectly on the landing and he straightened up to look back, counting fourteen steps. *How the hell?* He just jumped fourteen steps.

He studied his hands again, flipping them over then touching his torso, wondering how he just done that so effortlessly. Never would he have thought he could do that. Then again, he had never tried before either. Maybe he was a lot tougher than he assumed. He never had a problem with coordination. In boot camp he scaled the board-up walls with ease.

He could climb the side of his uncle's trailers without a ladder. He heard a door open many flights up. He needed to get out of there fast. Mindful of the door this time, he opened it slowly and scanned the lobby, quickly spotting Clair. In a couple of quick steps he was in front of her, glancing around for his dad suspiciously like someone was after him.

"Come on, let's get out of here. Now!"

Clair observed his paranoid expression and felt his firm grip as he held onto her upper arm, moving her in the direction of the exit. He was clearly alarmed. She didn't understand what was going on.

"What happened?"

"Damn it! Where is he?!" His eyes wildly searched the lobby.

"He's outside. Your dad. Outside." She pointed.

Pike released her upper arm and grabbed her wrist in urgency. She followed, keeping up with his pace.

Kris was on his phone, standing out front, watching traffic pass by on the main street.

"Let's go, dad!" Pike rushed by in a blur, releasing Clair's wrist. She rubbed where he had pulled. Her whole arm ached, but she managed to keep up with him stride for stride. Pike looked back to see if anyone was following them.

"What did she say?" Clair asked, now jogging to keep up.

"She's fleecing the insurance company."

"What?"

"They cut her a check for ten grand after she listed all the made-up furniture and clothing she lost."

"Did she say anything about the furniture?"

"Yes. After I confronted her about it. She said she has it. It's in storage."

"Why did she take it?"

"Said it was for us to start somewhere else."

Clair wanted more answers. "She listed the furniture that she took as the stuff she lost in the explosion? Pike? Come on. Doesn't that sound even more suspicious?"

Kris stopped, catching his breath, "Did you ask her about the stove?"

Pike tensed. His body temperature rose again and he pulled hard at his shirt collar, letting some of the heat out while as washed over him. "Yes."

Clair stopped in better shape than Kris, but still breathing heavier that Pike. Kris's eyebrows furrowed. "Well?"

"She wouldn't answer, but she might as well have. I could tell by the way she was avoiding the question. You were right. That's probably why she stored the furniture."

Kris turned back and began marching toward the entrance. "That little bitch."

Pike darted to him, grabbing his arm. Kris looked down at Pike's hold on him.

"Dad, we need to get out of here. Right now!"

Pike released his grip and Kris rubbed his arm from the pain. "Jesus, boy."

Pike curled his fingers, shaking his hands and growling in frustration over this physical change. He wasn't trying to hurt anyone. Clair watched him as he stomped quickly back toward the car. Kris held his arm and met Clair's bewildered gaze, matching her expression, before she nodded in the direction of the car for Kris to follow.

For the Greater Good

CLAIR ARGUED WITH PIKE, "Look, I am just saying. Don't claim anything. Tell the insurance company you didn't lose anything. They already paid Jackie. Do you need the money?"

"That's not the point. It's the principle of it. She takes and takes and takes."

"Donate her shit to charity. Don't ever see her again. Win-win. She has enough to move on. Kris, what do you think?"

"The girl blew up my house."

"Besides that. Am I right? This is a way for Pike to get her out of his life for good."

"Let's see what the insurance company says."

Pike sat brooding, watching the scenery rush past the passenger's side window. *Jackie,* he shook his head, *how could she? She stole from dad's house, blew it up, and now she ends up with bank?* Pike exited the car as soon as Kris shifted the gear into park. He paced until his father cleared the front of the LTD and they all started walking toward the entrance of the multi-story, beautifully designed building. The entrance was sterile and enormous, the lobby spotless and bright. A few chairs lined a seating area, and there was a receptionist desk with two women and a guard waiting behind the dark wood-paneled station to greet them as they neared. Kris announced his and Pike's name and let them know who he had an appointment with. Clair excused herself, pointing toward the seating area where she would wait. Pike nodded. She reassured him with a simple thumbs up.

His father handed Pike a visitor's badge, and they walked to the number four elevator. An older woman greeted them on the eighth floor, escorting them down the hall into a small conference room, asking if they wanted anything to drink. Pike wanted water. She pulled out a water from the mini fridge against the wall. "Mrs. Wheeler will be right in. Please take a seat."

Pike thanked her as Kris looked around at the expensive furniture and artwork. "Let the girl keep the money. This is why our insurance is so expensive." Pike and Kris took their seats. Mrs. Wheeler knocked, poking her head in, careful not to surprise them.

Kris stood up straight out of his chair, not expecting Mrs. Wheeler to be the stunning brunette walking toward him. He offered his hand. "If we video chatted when I first spoke with you Monday morning, I would have been here Monday afternoon."

"Oh? Thank you for coming all the way from Florida, Mr. Evans. Did you fly or drive?"

Kris smiled. "Drove. Picked up my boy here in North Carolina. He just graduated. Finally has a decent job. Government agent, so no funny business."

Mrs. Wheeler smiled, impressed as she shook Pike's hand. "Congratulations." She motioned for them to sit again while she spread her folders out in front of her. "We took care of Miss Smith's claim last night. Since Mr. Evans has been in North Carolina for the past month, are we looking to compensate for Massachusetts or North Carolina housing?"

Pike waved his hand out just above the table. "I don't need any compensation."

She glanced up from the open folder. "Nothing?"

"I have everything I own in North Carolina. Jackie was living at the house alone."

"Are you sure? Housing? It says you have a vehicle?"

"Safe with me in North Carolina. I'm good."

She put down her paperwork. "Are you sure, Mr. Evans? Furniture? A box of childhood memories?"

Pike shook his head. "It was Jackie's stuff. I have everything I want in North Carolina."

She tilted her head briefly before focusing back on the paperwork. "Okay, Mr. Evans, I need you to sign this form then." She slid it over to him. He picked up a fancy pen from the metal holder in the center of the table. Pike signed then pushed it back toward her. He could see clearly why Jackie did what she did. This woman was handing out free money. She wanted to pay. No questions asked.

He watched and waited to hear what she was going to offer Kris. His father tapped Pike's arm, motioning for them to switch seats. Kris now sat next to Mrs. Wheeler. "What do you have for me, sugar?"

Her thin smile revealed she was putting up with the way Kris was speaking to her. She collected the paper Pike had just signed, inserting it into her folder. She pulled papers out from another divider. "Mr. Evans. From everything you described over the phone, does this look like an accurate list?"

She pushed the two pages across the desk until they came to a stop under his left fingertips. He pulled them closer, reading over the first page and flipped the paper to read the second. He looked at the bottom figure. "Thirty-three thousand?"

"That's for the contents."

"How much for the house? It's been paid off for years."

She slid over another paper. "This is what they appraised the house for."

Once again, his fingers pulled the paper in front of him. He sucked in a breath at the price then went bug-eyed at her. She kept it professional. "That would be for the house and the lot. We will take over full ownership."

"How much if I stay and rebuild?"

Pike moved his dad's hand to see what they were offering. Six hundred and seventy-five thousand. "Dad!"

He stopped Pike from speaking. Staring at Mrs. Wheeler. She folded her hands in front of her. "We are not considering the option to rebuild."

Kris scrunched his face. "Why?"

She grinned warily. "Is the offer not acceptable?"

Kris picked up the paper. "This is more than the place is worth. Why don't I have the option to rebuild and keep it?"

"Mr. Evans. I apologize for not being able to disclose further information. The only thing I can do is tell them you are rejecting their offer and see if they come back with a different number."

"'Them?' Who is 'them?'"

"Dad, take the money."

"'Them' meaning this insurance company? What are you guys going to do with it?"

Mrs. Wheeler, on the edge of annoyance, inhaled slowly, her eyes staring into Kris's. Her breath expanded her chest pushing through her shirt. Kris's eyes darted straight to her chest, watching the buttons struggle out of alignment. "Mr. Evans. You have two options. You can accept or reject this offer. That's all I am authorized to discuss with you."

"Fine. Where do I sign."

Mrs. Wheeler smiled; chest still pushed out. "Maybe you could buy a place in North Carolina? Be near your son?"

Pike's eyes widened. "Dad. I know the perfect area."

He picked up the pen that Pike had used, twitched his mouth to the right. "Later, boy."

He pushed back the paperwork as Mrs. Wheeler reached, leaning her body forward, giving Kris a cleavage tease. "If you will wait a few minutes, I will have both checks for you."

She excused herself from the room, closing the door behind her. Pike grinned. "How much did you pay for the house?"

"One eighty-nine."

"That's over three times the value. You'll never get close to that amount. Especially in that neighborhood. I can see maybe in Hadley, but not Agawam."

"Who do you think *they* are?"

"Who knows? Who cares? They will never get back that kind of investment. The only thing that could make any money on that lot is a cell tower. Mrs. Johnson will never allow that."

Kris narrowed his eyes in suspicion. "Cell tower. That's interesting."

Mrs. Wheeler returned and politely smiled, handing Kris two envelopes. "It was a pleasure meeting you, Mr. Evans." She shook Kris's hand, then switched to Pike. "Mr. Evans."

Pike felt at ease about the whole insurance thing now. Jackie could keep his share of the money. Right now was the right time to break all ties with her. Clair was right. All her clothes could go charity down there. He didn't need to send her anything. Clair spotted them walking off the elevator. She studied Pike, concerned about what had happened to him in there as she met them halfway, eager to hear results. "Is everything okay? How did it go?"

Pike slowed as Clair fell in beside him. He rested his hand against her lower back, and she didn't seem to mind the contact.

"I didn't say anything. That woman was handing out money though. I can see why Jackie took her for everything she could get."

"What did you settle for?"

"I didn't. Jackie took enough for the both of us. I see it as a settlement between me and her. I'm done. Hey, Dad?" Pike angled his head toward his farther. "There is no reason to stay here. Can we check out and hit the road?"

Kris looked at his watch. "Sure. We are stopping in Maryland for crab though."

Clair's grin was angelic. "We can bring some back with us. Invite Kittrick and Captain Jacobowski. We need a do-over for your graduation dinner that was interrupted."

Pike beamed. "I would like that."

Clair stopped Pike. "I am glad you are closing the Jackie chapter."

"Me too."

Second Time a Charm.

THEY BOUGHT ENOUGH crab for a party of eight and packed it up tight in a temporary cooler for the five and a half hours left to complete the last leg of their journey. The Crab Shack provided samples. Clair insisted on no more sampling for Pike, making him sad, but she convinced him it would ruin their crab bake.

Pike didn't think so. He could eat crab meat for weeks and not complain. But to avoid argument, he gave in after one more sampling. Pike and Clair took the back seat. She wanted him to talk about what had happened back at the hotel, but he wasn't talking so she initiated by sharing a story, hoping he would open up. She talked about when she and Hanskon were together and happy.

"I took on a last-minute armored run, Texas to Kentucky. They flew me out and he was different. Actually, he was pissed-off from the moment I exited the plane. Mind you, we hadn't seen each other for a month, so it wasn't the reaction I was expecting. Come to find out, I was Dee Dee Kahnawake's replacement."

Pike wanted to know these things and leaned in. "Who was she?"

"His girlfriend."

"Did you break up?"

Clair turned her head for a moment, watching the twilight settle in for the evening.

Pike cupped her shoulder. She turned to face him. "It took me years to smarten up. I don't want that for you, and I see it playing out. Jackie is just as manipulating as he was."

"Why does your family want you to end up with him then?"

"Eli."

"Your half-brother?"

"He is Eli's right-hand man."

Pike grinned. "To jerk him off?"

Clair chuckled. "Maybe?"

"I don't get it. Your mother, does she know what went on?"

"She doesn't care."

"About you being happy? Being able to trust your partner?"

"In her eyes, it's because women belong at home, making babies and taking care of their men."

Pike sat back. "That's a load of bullshit. Your own mother is a hypocrite. What about the shrine for Eli's dad? Doesn't she know how that must make your dad feel?"

"I am sure she does. Probably the reason why she does it."

"That's brutal."

"Know what's brutal?"

"What?"

"I actually think she regrets marrying him and having me."

"Jesus."

Clair turned her head again, thinking about what she had finally admitted out loud. Pike touched her knee. "Well, doesn't matter what she thinks. I am glad you are here."

She turned her head again, looking down and watching his fingers resting on her before following them up to his gaze. "You better not fuck up my driving status."

He chuckled, withdrawing his touch. "You better not fuck up mine." Both of them chuckled. Pike didn't want to end their moment. Clair hadn't shared much about what had happened between Hanskon and herself. He tried to hint at where he wanted this to go. "Nowadays, it takes two working people to contribute financially."

"Like Jackie did?"

Pike readjusted in his seat. "Whoa, that wasn't where I was going."

"Sorry." She encouraged him to continue.

"I mean, if you want a nice house, family."

Kris interrupted, "Your mother said the road was not a way to raise kids."

Pike's jaw dropped. "Wait a minute. Those were my best memories. I loved my summers traveling. The stuff you and Uncle Wade let me do . . ." Pike snickered with a grin spreading ear to ear. "I want my kids to have that."

Kris's eyes watched Pike's expression. "They will never have it with you working for the government. Do you think that Captain Jacobowski will let you strap a baby seat in those rigs?"

Pike's smile lessened but was still there. "I'll figure that out when it happens."

Kris segued to Wade's estate. "You know, Pike, Wade wanted you to have the farm. It's been sitting there. Those trucks need attention."

Clair sat forward, intrigued. "What farm?"

Pike tried squashing the conversation. "Rundown place in Virginia. Middle of nowhere."

Clair grinned. "Bootleg country?"

Pike smiled back. "Yup."

She nodded. "Cool."

Kris encouraged the curiosity. "You two should go visit it. Assess what the place needs."

Pike turned his head, looking at his dad's eyes in the rearview. "Needs for what?"

"Make it what it should be. Your uncle wanted you to have it. It's your home, Pike."

"Does that mean I can sell it and buy something near the base?"

"No. It's got too much value and would attract the wrong people."

Pike scooched forward. "What does that mean?"

Kris held the steering wheel with both hands. "Means it's not for sale."

Pike slid back. "That makes no sense."

"As long as I am alive, that place is not for sale."

Clair nudged Pike hard enough for him to see a *don't go there* signal. He frowned, so she changed the subject. "What happened back at the hotel?"

That shut him up the rest of the drive back.

Home is Where the Condo is.

IT WAS CLOSE TO MIDNIGHT, and they were finally back at Clair's condo complex. Pike pulled the cooler from the trunk with Clair halting him to drain out the excess water. She added the two bags of ice they had purchased at the gas station down the road on the final stop for the night.

She nodded, satisfied. "That should keep the crabs safe overnight."

Pike smirked. "You have a refrigerator?"

Smacking his arm, she protested, "Hey, trust me. This is the way to go."

"I think you like torturing me so the crabs won't defrost."

She fought off a half-smile, shrugging. "Maybe? We still need to cook them."

It was obvious as all three sets of eyes peered into Pike's car that Kris and Clair were trying not to comment on all of Jackie's stuff packed in the back. Something for Pike to decide on tomorrow.

They focused back on the cooler and on getting their bags inside. Pike insisted the cooler, holding seven bags of ice and crabs for eight, was no big deal as he carried it with ease inside her condo. She followed behind, observing how heavy that must have been as she carried their overnight bags.

Clair played hostess. "Kris, would you like the guest bed upstairs?"

Pike's eyebrows suddenly raised. That was his room. Then realized how rude he was being. "Go ahead, Dad. I am good down here. As a matter of fact, I am surprised she hasn't made me sleep down here from the start." He faintly laughed at his joking. Clair moved her hand to her hip and flexed one eyebrow as she stared at him. "Me too. I gotta rethink the sleeping arrangements for the future."

His hand shot out. "Kidding. I am only kidding with you. I like the bed upstairs."

She hmphed. "That's what I thought. But seriously, Kris, you are more than welcome to it for the remainder of your stay."

"Couch suits me just fine. Thanks though. Appreciate it, Clair."

She was satisfied he had turned it down because he liked the couch. She joked with Pike. "Guess it's all yours then." He wasn't waiting for her to change her mind and make him sleep on the recliner again. He picked up both their bags and headed upstairs.

The towels on the floor made Clair think about pulling it off from Jackie's hair. Then she realized Jackie was the last one in the guest bed. She insisted on changing the sheets before Pike could settle in. Pike tried to stop her, but Clair was not having his being reminded of Jackie in her own home. The sheets were changed and thrown downstairs in front of the wash for tomorrow.

It was almost one o'clock in the morning – time to rest. Pike, in his room again, lay there looking up at the ceiling. *That was a lot of commotion about changing the sheets.* He rolled to the side with the delicate fragrance from Clair's laundry detergent. *Maybe she had a point*, he thought, before drifting off to sleep.

Saturday morning, Pike woke hearing Clair close the bathroom door. His eyes opened wide. *No, no, no, no.* There was movement under the sheets. He jumped out of bed, pushing his manhood down. "Not now. Fack." He listened. No shower. "Fack." The bathroom door opened, and he scrambled for how to handle this. Jumping jacks! He called out, "One, two, three, four, five, six!" It was working. There was a knock on his door before Clair opened it without an invite.

"Hey. You're up. Nice. I didn't know you like to exercise in the morning." She smiled as Pike spun around and grabbed his coat holding it in front of him.

She opened the door wider. "You know we can go to the gym. I'm in. I like working out in the mornings." What the hell was he doing? She focused on the coat and pointed. "You going somewhere?"

He scrambled, keeping the front part of himself in the opposite direction of her. He dropped the coat, keeping his back to her as he maneuvered his way past her and out of the bedroom. "You done in the bathroom?" His voice was unsteady.

She watched. "Um, yes? Why are you acting all weird?"

Still angling his back toward her, he'd nearly made it to the bathroom. "I need a shower." Safely behind the door, he turned and smiled guiltily. "Be right down." He pointed at the stairs.

Clair's brows raised, full of suspicion as he closed the door. Pike reasoned with his manhood, which was still standing ready for action. "Dude, now? Not the time." He heard Clair comment from the other side of the door, "Might want to make it a cold one."

He faintly whispered, "Good idea."

The shower got Pike back in control, and he dressed in his jeans and white t-shirt. No uniform today. It was their last weekend before his official start as agent on Monday. Clair, feeling her own appreciation for how her new partner filled out his casuals, whispered under her breath, "Damn."

Kris was awake, sitting at the table and talking to Clair, who was across the room starting laundry. Pike walked straight to the coffee machine, avoiding eye contact with Clair. Apparently, they were talking about the land value of Kris's plot. "This doesn't make sense."

Pike started to regret not showing Clair around Massachusetts some more and promised to take her back at Thanksgiving when she could meet his mother's side of the family. Kris rocked forward out of the kitchen chair adding, "Good luck with that."

They delayed cleaning the patio area until 9:00 a.m. Pike's first job was vacuuming the furniture. He made sure everything would pass Clair's inspection. He wanted to make sure she realized she could count on him for whatever she needed done. After the patio windows were clean, the outside was ready for guests. Pike admired his work and asked, "What about one of those fire pits?"

She twisted her lips, staring out at the lawn. "Never thought about getting one for here. My parents have one. It's pretty cool in the evenings. My father and I had some intense conversations when everyone went inside, and it was just the two of us left. The warmth from the fire, cool night."

Pike smiled. "See, we should buy one."

Turning her head from the spot she thought would be a good location, she took in his expression. He was very happy about the idea. "Maybe." She decided that was as good an answer as any and motioned for them to finish up inside.

Clair, seeing how far she could push him, asked him to put the next load of laundry on. When he walked away without saying a word and clearly in the direction of her request, she couldn't help but observe how easy-going he really was. Not one complaint over any of the housework she had asked him to do. He was on it.

Pike conversed with his dad, who had claimed the recliner and was watching The Weather Channel. Pike transferred the wash into the dryer, while convincing Kris this was where he would like to settle, not in Virginia at Uncle Wade's place, triggering a pent-up argument that sounded like it had been buried forever.

"The plan was for you to take over keeping the place up and taking care of the trucks."

"It's in the middle of nowhere."

"It's worth a lot of money."

"Can I sell it?"

"In sentimental value too."

"You move there then. It's your childhood farm."

"I can't."

"You can't? Why?"

"Never mind why. It's yours to take care of. That's what he wanted."

Pike stopped pressing his dad about Uncle Wade's request. Clair grinned, walking toward them. "Bet you were a hellraiser in that town."

Kris softened. "Something like that."

Clair listened to The Weather Channel Kris watched as she made out a list of what they needed for the party. She wasn't used to entertaining and was kind of into it. Since this was her first party, she wanted everything perfect. She smiled, listening to Kris and Pike complain about the A&M Transport and how it was the worst company Kris had ever worked for – everything from broken trucks to broken owners.

Clair was amused by the stories they swapped. Pike was around ten at the time. Clair was impressed by how much he remembered. She stood up, carrying over her list. "So what is your earliest childhood memory?"

He tilted his head. "I remember feeling sick, and I was going to puke, and we didn't have anything, so Dad handed me the urinal."

Clair's hands shot up, covering her mouth as she laughed. "Yeah, Mom was horrified. I think that prompted the Agawam house." Kris stopped watching the news. "You were three? You remember that?"

"Yeah. She scrubbed my mouth so hard and brushed my teeth for ten minutes. I will never forget that. My mouth hurt for the rest of the day."

"On that note, let's show your dad around. I have to pick up a few things." It was the perfect segue to offering to drive Kris around for a quick tour of the area. Maybe seeing what was around here would soften him up.

Pikes relaxed his shoulders, dropping them back down to where they should be resting. Why was he so intense when he was talking with his father? Kris turned off the television and stood. "You can show me around, but don't think it's going to replace that hidden gem in Virginia."

They hopped in her Jeep. Pike glanced inside his car at the bags of clothes Jackie had brought. Clair saw him staring as she watched in her rearview. "Hey."

Pike turned, giving her his attention in her mirror. "I'll take care of those if you want me to."

He nodded. "Thanks."

Driving around Fayetteville was not the same adventure for Kris as was impressing Pike. He could picture himself settling here. Kris commented again that he was hoping Pike would settle in Virginia. Clair, once again breaking the tension that was building, asked, "What part of Florida are you in?"

He nodded. "Nine hours with stops."

"Oh, so you are in the nine-hour part?"

Kris chuckled. "Yes."

Clair spun his game. "Well, lucky you. It's only a day's drive to here. Virginia adds a few more hours and then the whole day is gone."

Kris narrowed his eyes at her. "Oh, you are a slippery one."

They pulled in the parking lot to the store. Without another word, Pike volunteered to go in and gather the things on the list. This would give Clair some private time to talk with Kris. She handed Pike the list. "Stick to the list."

He nodded. "Yes, She Who Must Be Obeyed."

Clair chuckled. "I like that."

Kris watched Pike grinning as he turned and walked away. That was how he referred to Kim behind her back. Pike was playful with Clair.

"You know, Morris, my boy hasn't had a lot of positive female influence. My former wife is about as controlling as they come."

"Saw that on first impression."

"Then this Jackie. She had him wrapped around her finger."

"Yeah, that's obvious."

"What's your angle?"

"Angle?"

"I can see something there."

"Then look away. We are just partners." She watched the entrance to the store, wondering if she should go in.

She decided to stay and argue as she turned the conversation back to Kris. "How far away from an airport would Pike be in Virginia? I'm just asking because location is key with our job."

"We could make an airport on the family land."

"Then he needs a pilot."

"I was hoping Pike would bring that place to life again. Been sitting for too long. It's worth its weight in gold. I can see him here, settling down, raising a family." Kris turned, directing this to Clair. "What do you think about Virginia?"

"Hang on, worth its weight in gold? Is there a mine? Is that why?"

"Sentimentally speaking."

"I think I am the wrong person to ask. I like it here. Kittrick would be thrilled. He lives in Virginia, on the coast next to the base."

Kris rubbed his chin. "Right. Forgot about that."

"So, you know Agent Kittrick?"

"We go aways back."

"You're kidding me."

"Trucking is a small industry, sweetheart. Or at least it was back in the day."

"Do you still drive?"

"Only when I have to."

"I mean rigs?"

"Like I said, only when I have to."

"I'm not sure what that means."

"It means I've been doing this a long time. If I am going to drive, then the incentive must be large."

She smiled. "That's cool. What do you do in Florida?"

"Drive my boat. Fish. Give private tours."

"Like deep sea fish?"

"Not that deep. I stay close to the mainland. People love to look at all the rich folks' houses."

"Ever get any reports from those trash magazines asking you?"

"You would be surprised how much they pay."

"Really? You do that?"

"Money is money."

Clair eyed Kris in a different light now. "Don't you think that's an invasion of privacy?"

"No."

She didn't like the way this conversation was going. "Tell me about the place in Virginia."

"Pike grew up there in the summers. That kid had more energy. Driving kept him focused. He learned real fast."

"How old was he when he started?"

"Much younger than he was allowed."

"Uncle Wade's. Is that the same place?"

"He talked about Wade?"

"Only that he taught Pike to do some truck tricks. Pike's driving has been very impressive over the past month."

"In Wade's business, manipulating a rig was a necessity."

"What was his business?"

Kris explored Clair's face. This was a simple enough question for a typical person. Clair was not typical. She drove heavily classified containers for a living. "Driving."

She chuckled. "No shit. Figured that one out on my own."

Kris didn't expect her to answer him like that. "I like you, Morris."

"I want to hear more stories about Pike. Need ammo for when he gets on my nerves driving."

The right side of his face turned up. "My son is good at that."

Pike walked out grinning. "Got everything on the list plus something for the host."

She peeked in the bag, spotting the cookies she liked. Clair approved. "Good thinking. Will make it easier putting up with the two of you for the rest of Daddy Evans' stay."

Pike chuckled. "My thoughts exactly."

"See how the storm dictates. Might head out tomorrow."

"Really?"

"Yes."

Pike pulled his phone out. It was Jackie's number. She didn't know they left yesterday. He let it go to voicemail. "What do you think about Fayetteville now, Dad?"

"I think it's the same as when I arrived."

Pike checked the phone again. "We have two hours before the party starts."

Clair glanced in her rearview mirror. "Plenty of time."

"I've never cooked crab before." Pike admitted.

"No worries, Evans. I am a pro." She grinned in the rearview.

His phone vibrated again. His mother this time. "Hey, Mom."

"What are you doing tonight?"

He made a lopsided smile. "We are back in North Carolina. Everything straightened out with the insurance, so we left as soon as Dad got the checks."

"How much did they give him?"

"I think that is a question you should ask him yourself."

"Did they give you anything?"

"No. I turned down any money."

"What! Why?"

"Because none of my stuff was worth anything."

"Something would have been better than nothing. Now you have to go out and buy all that stuff."

"I've got all I need down here. I'm making good money. I am all set."

"I wish I could have seen you one last time before you headed back."

"Sorry about that."

"I liked meeting your partner. She's mature and responsible enough to keep you in line."

"Huh? What does that mean?"

"It means watch yourself and behave."

"I need to tell you that Jackie is back there. If you see her just leave her alone. We broke up, and I don't want her to have to reach out to me over something you did."

"Why would you say such a thing? Of course, I will leave her alone. She is out of your life for good, right?"

"Yes."

"Then she is free to go about her business."

"I gotta go, Mom."

"Call me next week?"

"I will." Pike hung up, muttering under his breath.

Kris turned his head. "That your mother?"

"Ha, how'd you guess."

"She asking how much I got for the place?"

"Yes."

"Nosy woman."

"I told her to ask you."

"Heard that. Appreciate it."

Crab Bake North Carolina Style

CLAIR FILLED THE BIGGEST pot she had with water and let it sit on the stove to a rolling boil. She dropped the crabs in one at a time. Pike covered his ears, "Jesus Christ! What is that?"

Clair was puzzled. "What?"

Pike ran out of the condo with his hands over his ears. It took the distance of his car for the noise to become bearable. He searched everywhere. Up, down, side to side, looking around for the source. Then it stopped.

Kris walked out. "Everything okay?"

Pike stepped toward his dad, still alarmed. "You didn't hear that?"

"Hear what?"

"That deafening screech."

"I didn't hear anything."

Clair stood at the door. "What was that all about?"

"I heard this sound. Hurt my ears." He walked back to Clair. She stopped him and turned his head. "Your ear is bleeding."

"What?" He touched the inside of this right ear and a tiny drop of blood smeared his fingertip. "What the hell?"

"Does it hurt?"

"No. Not at all."

"Come here. I'll get you some ice."

Pike shook his head, tilting it to the right. It was just that one small droplet. Nothing else appeared. Clair handed him a towel filled with ice. "Press this against your ear."

Gus and Maggie arrived together. She held a small, rectangular box with a bow on top. "What's wrong with your ear?"

He shrugged. "Strangest thing. One second I'm watching Clair drop the crabs in the water and then this incredibly loud pitch attacks my ears. I had to cover them and run out. It was at my car that I could finally bear it. Clair noticed when I came back in there was a little blood."

She handed 49 the present and pulled out a pocket flashlight. Pike lowered the ice cloth and she peered inside. "No blood now?"

He shrugged again. "Weird?"

"You feel okay?"

"Fine."

"Okay, I'll note this. We will keep an eye on it. Maybe you have a middle ear infection or something?"

"I feel perfectly fine."

"Still, better safe than sorry."

49 ate two crabs all on his own, smacking his lips and licking his fingertips. "Now this was a good idea. Who thought about bringing home Maryland crab?"

Kris grinned. "The girl, of course. We fellas don't think about stuff like that."

Clair looked at the leftovers. "Looks like we have a few options for leftovers."

Captain Jacobowski offered, "I have a great recipe for crab cakes."

49 rubbed his hands. "I like the sound of that."

Pike casually pointed his index finger at 49. "I'm not sure that's on your diet."

"Oh hush up, kid."

Kris sat back, studying Gus and Pike. "They got you on some special diet, Gus?"

Pike blurted out before thinking, "Yes, they tend to do that after a heart attack."

Kris sat forward. "You had a heart attack?"

Pike grew quiet and sheepishly looked at 49 to judge his reaction. He felt bad about spilling the beans, but not entirely. He cared about 49, and this was important.

Pike looked at his father. "The day I met this guy. He was on the side of the road having a heart attack just outside of the city limits of Agawam."

Kris grinned. "Apparently you lived. I want to hear this story. About time one of you told it."

Pike snickered. "My version is way better. I'll tell him." They all picked at their crab as they listened to Pike's version of 49 nearly clipping his produce truck on the way to the day's first delivery.

49 countered, "I didn't nearly hit your truck. I was miles away."

Pike pointed and laughed. "Dude, I had to slam on my brakes or you would have taken my front end out."

49 dug out a small piece of white meat, bringing it to his mouth, "Your boy exaggerates. Definitely a family trait."

Kris laughed. "Must get it from his mother."

Pike grinned. "Next thing I know he's reciting *For God and Country*. I couldn't leave him. My mornings were filled with same shitty problems, one after another, for weeks at a time back home. When I looked in the cab it was set up like command central. Way better than the piece of crap parked behind him. So I went along for the ride."

"What about that produce company?" asked Kris.

"My boss would yell at me for being fifteen minutes early that I didn't get paid for. He was an asshole. Guy wanted free labor and made us clock in after the trucks were loaded. At $18 an hour . . . there was nothing keeping me there except the free food."

Clair sat back. "Even though you were pretty annoying when you arrived, I'm glad you took the chance."

"Annoying? Me?"

She smirked, butting her boot against his, making him show teeth with his grin.

Captain Jacobowski glanced around for the gift. "Gus, where did . . . ?" She spotted it on the counter and stood up retrieving the case. "I meant to give you this Wednesday, but with all the unexpected company arriving I didn't feel it was the time."

Pike reached for the box. "What is it?"

She grinned. "A little something."

He opened it to find a silver dog tag on a keyring. He flipped it over. There was an engraving. *ATG Evans*. Pike's eyes softened. "Wow. This is really nice. Thanks. What is ATG?"

"Assigned to Ghost."

His smile spread wide. "I am officially in the Ghost fleet?"

She grinned sarcastically. "I have no idea what you are talking about. It doesn't exist."

Pike quickly responded, "Don't ask questions and do as you are told."

49 let out a "Ha!" as Clair nodded. "Copy that." The captain shook her head and held in a laugh.

On Sunday, Pray.

"I HAVE TO GO TO CHURCH at ten."

Pike's craned his neck in response to Clair's words. "Um?"

Kris watched the news, more interested in a new tropical storm brewing off the coast that was quickly growing stronger. They were on the letter M. The experts had named it Maria. Kris muttered as Pike called from the morning dishes, "What did you say, dad?"

"Maria. I dated a girl named Maria. A walking disaster. Lord have mercy. This storm is going to be a disaster."

"Never heard you mention Maria before."

He turned up the volume on the television. "And for good reason. The woman was crazier than a bag of cats."

Pike laughed. Clair grinned and asked, "Did you get yourself a clinger?"

"She knitted me a hat. When in hell would I need a knit hat in Florida?"

Pike burst out laughing and pointed. "Guess she was hoping you would take her back to Massachusetts."

Kris grumbled under his breath. "She thought wrong."

Pike moved across the room, picking up the laundry basket after Clair finished folding. Everything was stacked in neat, folded piles on the sofa. He combined his stuff on the bottom and hers on top.

Clair watched. "You can set my stuff at the end of my bed."

"Be right back." He jogged up the stairs with Kris watching. "That girl probably made him do everything."

Clair grinned. "Lucky me."

Pike walked back down. "What are we doing today? It's my last day of freedom."

Clair shrugged. "Church in two hours."

Kris watched the television. "Say hi to the Lord for me. I'm happy right where I am."

Pike twisted his mouth. This was something he and Clair could do together. But it was church. He didn't have much experience going. "What religion are you?"

"Protestant."

"Is that a good one or bad one?"

She leaned her head to the side. "What?"

"Is it a religion that accepts people or keeps you under their thumb?"

"I'm not under anyone's thumb."

"Can I go with you?"

"You want to go to church?"

"It's my first Sunday that I have a choice besides the gun range."

Clair tapped her fingers on the table next to her coffee. "Let me think about it."

Pike watched her fingers. "Oh, come on. I can't screw up church."

She stopped tapping, suddenly realizing what he was looking at. She grabbed her coffee mug. "Yes, you can."

"Dude!"

She bounced her knee. Pike took the seat next to her, folding his hands and resting them on the table. "That's fine, if you don't want me to go. Just pretend I never asked." He turned toward the television.

Clair sighed. "It's not you. My parents go. I don't want to give them the wrong impression."

Pike wasn't sure how to take that. "Wrong impression? I would think they'd be happy I wanted to attend."

She shook her head. "Too complicated."

Pike gave up. "Fine. I'll go explore this area then. Dad, want to drive around with me?"

Kris grunted out in protest. "Again?"

Pike grunted back. "Unbelievable. It's all right, I'll go by myself." He texted 49 to see if he wanted to drive around with him. 49 replied right away and asked where he could pick him up. Clair left and Kris settled back into watching the NFL pre-game show.

Pike grabbed his sweatshirt and asked if he could bring anything back for his dad. Kris raised his hand as the TV displayed highlights from last week's games. "All set, boy. Don't get lost."

Pike approached his car and realized it was time for an upgrade. For the first time in his life, he could afford a new car payment. He picked up 49, who looked suspiciously at the car. "Is this okay to get into? Is there room?"

Pike frowned. "She's reliable. Brought Jackie here no problem from Massachusetts. Going to get rid of this stuff this week."

"If we break down you're the one who's going to call it in."

Pike reminded him to fasten his seatbelt. Car shopping became the agenda this afternoon. All of the lots were closed, so it was a good day to window shop. Pike was drawn to the muscle cars at first, until the sticker price kept making him cringe. He had to think about housing.

49 steered him to look at the economy models. He liked the price and looks of the Civic. Sporty yet practical. Leather seats. A sunroof. This was his car. He took a picture of the car, then the model number and sticker.

Clair was practical. Maybe he should look at the sporty ones. He could see her in the passenger seat. Wait a minute. It was Clair he was thinking about. He would be in the passenger seat.

Pike and 49 finished car shopping for the day and headed back for a tour around Fayetteville. "I like this area," Pike said. "And you, sir? How did you know to pick Virginia?"

"I didn't exactly pick Virginia. I'm there for other reasons."

Pike wiggled his eyebrows. "A woman?"

"No, nothing like that."

"Is it because of family?"

49 huffed. "One ghost in particular."

"Ghost? As in *boo!*?"

"Your father. What's his place like in Florida?"

"It's average. Two bedrooms, two baths. Looks like all the rest of the houses in the area. He has a big lot though. He could easily build another house on it."

"Keep his boat on his property?"

Pike twisted his lips. "Nah, the boat club takes care of it. He just has to show up and pop in his key. They take care of fuel, cleaning, maintenance. Besides, I don't think he would let a boat sit next to his car."

"That is a pristine vehicle. He's taken good care of it."

"He bought it two years ago. Cost more than that black Charger we just looked at."

"Is that so?"

"I don't get him sometimes. I would never waste money on an old clunker like that."

"Sounds like your dad has done pretty well for himself."

"And just got better. More than a half a million sitting in his pocket as we speak."

"Tell me more about your trip."

Car Payment Because Base Housing is Free.

PIKE HEADED FOR THE base with 49 to grab dinner. He liked the fact that he could still eat every meal here and not have to pay for it. He texted Clair, who was still at church. He looked at the time, happy she turned him down. He checked in with his dad who decided on round two of the great crab-fest. Looking down at his free burger and fries, he admitted they were pretty good too.

Pike inquired about the military housing option. Captain Jacobowski had put all the information together for him. Pike opened the folder and thought that if his father wouldn't give him a loan, at least base housing would be an solid backup plan. With Clair not letting him tag along to church, he thought he'd better keep his options open.

Tomorrow was going to be the test run on the new tractor trailer.

49 broke down the information about their road trip. It was going to be a simple run. One overnight between three drivers and back to base. Pike only needed to pack light. They were taking Cooper's test truck. "A simple run," 49 called it.

Rangers started to pile into the mess hall, still jacked up from jumping. Pike smiled and watched them banter. 49 put down his burger. "You know, kid . . ." he wiped his mouth, "You still have to learn how to jump."

Pike nodded toward the Rangers. "Judging by their reaction, I'm kind of looking forward to it."

As Pike watched the men, he thought of Miller and Vonn. He would have liked jumping with them. "When I learn, can we include the boys you first arranged?"

"Best leave that for Maggie to decide."

"Of course. Just didn't know, if I asked, if that was possible."

"I'll let her know your request."

"Thanks. But whatever she decides I am good with."

"Any problem with your ear today?"

Pike brought his hand up to touch his ear. "No. Forgot all about that."

"Strange."

"Tell me about it. I actually ran out of Clair's house covering my ears it hurt so much."

"From a sound?"

"Apparently from a sound no one else heard."

"Like a dog whistle?"

"Dog whistle?"

"Yeah, a dog whistle. The frequency is so high only dogs can hear."

"Never knew there was such a thing."

"I'll see if I can get my hands on one. We can test it out."

Pike shrugged. "I guess."

"Ever been sensitive in your hearing before?"

Pike shrugged. "No."

They finished their food. Pike offered, "Want to come back to the house? Watch some football?"

"Thanks, kid. You can drop me at my place. Need to check on a few things for tomorrow."

"What's it like living on base?"

"Easy. My home away from home. Everything I need is right here."

"Cost?"

"Don't pay anything."

"Really? I heard that, but didn't know if the cost was actually nothing."

"Told you that before. No money comes out of my pay, and it's my place."

"I know you did. Just thinking about that Charger. No living expenses will be a breeze to afford."

"It's up to you, but that Honda would be my choice. Especially driving up North for holidays."

"Oh. Good point."

"You have plenty of time to get a race car. Save your money to put toward a nice place of your own."

"Thanks for going with me today."

"Not a problem. Been so used to hanging out with you the past month, this was good."

"Yeah, thanks for being there to answer my call back in Mass. I appreciated it. What time in the morning, sir?"

"Six o'clock, kid."

"Argh. Okay."

When they got back, Clair had returned and was watching the game with Kris. Pike walked in and Clair looked up from the couch. "Hey, how'd it go?"

Pike set his information packet on the kitchen table. "I picked up 49 and we looked at cars."

"Really? You going to trade in yours?"

"Thinking about it."

"Did anything interest you?"

Pike chuckled. "Yes, but out of my price range. There is this new Honda I liked."

Kris nodded. "That's a reliable car."

Pike pulled out his phone, handing it to Clair. "This is it."

"Oh, nice. I like it. That's a decent price."

"I'm going to call the dealership tomorrow when we're on the road."

"Did Kittrick mention a time?"

Pike put his phone back in his sweatshirt pocket "Guess he's feeling better. We're back to a six o'clock start."

The opposing team scored a touchdown, drawing a string of curses from Kris.

"I like consistency," Clair said. "Six works great." She turned to Kris. "We're leaving tomorrow at five-thirty. You can stay or head out. Up to you. You're welcome here anytime."

"That works for me. I don't see this storm heading out to sea."

"Oh? Hey, if it doesn't, I can give you a key. Stay here. Don't drive in it."

"I don't see a garage in this complex?"

"No. Sorry."

"I'll have to think about that. Might head out in a few hours."

She turned to Pike. "You hungry? I made crab salad with some of the leftovers."

"Thanks," he put his hand over his stomach, "but I ate at the cafeteria with 49."

Kris heard that. "49? Who's is that?"

Clair chuckled. "That's what he calls Agent Kittrick."

"Where you get that from?"

Pike stood straight up from leaning over the couch. "That's all I could remember from his number when I first met him."

"Makes sense. You guys make everything complicated."

Clair smiled wide. "How so?"

"You have numbers and names and this and that."

She stood up. "It's not complicated. Besides, I prefer reporting my number than my name over the radio."

"What number they give you, boy?"

Pike already knew his by heart. "50399. Or, as I like to say, 99."

Options

HURRICANE MARIA WAS about to hit, with three major projected landfall targets. The news flashed across the bottom of the screen.

First was Florida's central east coast, followed by Georgia, and third, if the winds pushed it enough, the upper banks of North Carolina and Virginia, where 49 lived. That was enough confirmation for Kris to leave right after the game, with Clair packing him leftover crabmeat and sandwiches. He felt comfortable enough to give her a hug and stole a kiss on her cheek.

She smiled. "Text him when you get home so we know you made it."

He gave Clair a relaxed salute and patted Pike's arm. "Good work, son. I'll call you when I get there."

"Thanks for driving up."

"It was worth it . . . by more than half a million dollars." Kris winked and picked up his bag, heading out."

Pike folded the clothes he picked for the trip and packed them in his bag. Clair had hers ready next to the wall. He placed his next to hers.

Clair was on her computer, watching the storm. "We won't be affected at all. Rest of the country looks good. I can't even imagine driving tomorrow with blue tires. Bet our rig gets tagged all over social media."

"I think the tires are cool. I wonder what the purpose is though. Cooper said he perfected the formula."

"What's the purpose? Attract attention."

"I suppose he could use that as a diversion. You know, hey, look over here at this strange and wonderful thing while we are doing something really bad over there."

Clair's eyes widened. "That's it."

"I'm kidding."

"No, really. That could be it exactly."

"No, really. I was just kidding."

"That makes more sense than actually carrying cargo. We drive decoy containers all the time. Why not make a decoy really flashy?"

"Why not? The government wouldn't bother, that's why."

"Wouldn't bother? Do you know how much they pay Neumann?"

"Cooper?"

"Yeah."

"He's a scientist, right?"

"That kid makes just shy of four million a year."

"What? No."

"Yes. Look at the past few weeks. Our runs were retrieving stuff for him. With guards."

"Not the stuff at Lejeune?"

"But we picked it up from Lejeune."

Pike laughed from the thought popping up in his brain. "Probably duct tape."

"Not funny."

"So what? He's super smart. He deserves the money, then. I couldn't do what he does."

"I'm just saying. Wait, what were we talking about?"

"Distraction."

She shifted in her seat as she typed on her keyboard. "They would pay a whole lot of money to get away with something that would or could cost them more."

"Keep talking, Clair. You're making me feel really good about transporting for them now."

"Simple, straightforward, benefits, good pay, and lots of time off. It's as good a job as any."

"I remember 49 mentioning you wanted to buy an RV?"

She turned her head, smiling. "I do. Hopefully next spring."

"That's cool."

"Dad's retiring in four years. He and I always talked about visiting all the national parks."

"Just you and your dad?"

"Me and Pop. Give him a break from mom."

"I would ask why, but after meeting them I completely understand."

"She spends most of the summer with Eli and Scottie. I have five weeks off. Dad and I could get some good sightseeing in."

"How does that work?" Pike continued. "Since we're partners now, do we have to take the same time off?"

Clair tipped her head. "Hmm. Don't think so. Would imagine one of us will always have to be available."

Pike's phone vibrated. He pulled it from his pocket. Jackie. Clair studied his reaction. "Don't tell me it's her?"

"It is."

Clair turned back to her computer. "Stay strong, buddy."

Pike walked up the stairs placing his phone on the dresser. Why was she still calling? There was a voice message this time. Could be information on the furniture she took. It didn't matter now. Everything was all settled with the insurance company. He wasn't going to tell anyone about her fraud.

Clair planned to donate all her clothing. That could be what she was calling about. He kept glancing at his phone. It wouldn't hurt to hear her message. No one would know that he listened. Pike distracted himself for a minute, looking around for anything else he would need for the trip.

He could take a shower. That would be enough time to squash his curiosity. He called down to Clair, "Hey, mind if I jump in the shower?"

She was standing at the bottom of the stairs. "Yah, sure. I'm going to catch up on some paperwork then head to bed. Probably setting my alarm for four. We'll head out at five-thirty?"

He nodded. "Sounds good." She walked away. "Hey, Clair?"

There she was again. "What? You need me to fill your bath?"

He smirked. "No. Just want to thank you for letting my dad stay and coming up to Agawam with us. I am glad you were there."

She nodded. "No problem. I like your parent. Dad. Looks like we are in the same boat with our mothers."

"They were both glad to meet you. Dad was comfortable here. I'm going to head to bed after. I'll get up after you're done in the bathroom."

"We will eat on base?"

"Yes. Sounds good." He tapped on the wall and turned.

Blue Tires

Clair wasn't exactly the quietest person waking up. Doors closing and opening. Bare feet padding to her room then back to the bathroom. Back and forth. Back and forth.

Pike lay there, eyes open, struggling to ignore another erection. Finally, he heard the shower turn on. He rolled over and considered his two options. First, he could go downstairs and take care of it in the other bathroom. Or second, he could stay right here and will it away. He picked up his phone. Now was as good as any time to listen to Jackie's message. Instant mood killer. That did the trick.

"Pike. I thought about what you said. Monday I am going to contact the insurance lady and give the money back. I did it for us. I saw it as my way of contributing. I planned on giving you the money for a down payment on a place for us and then we would have the furniture too. I really want to make this work. I will get a job down there. Let me prove it to you. I don't want to be here anymore. Okay, call me. I love you."

His emotions stirred and his heart thumped a little faster. The sheets smelled like Clair's laundry detergent. There was a slight ringing in his ear. He heard a car door close and immediately flung the covers off. *That had better not be her!* He separated the slats in the blinds, searching the parking lot. It was a man, coming off the night shift, from the looks of him, and carrying a satchel over his shoulder. He pointed his hand to the car as it lit up with a quick beep. Pike let go of the slats and backed toward the bed. He sat.

Pike picked up his phone and stared at the message, his heart rate dropping with a thud. He regretted yelling at her. He had pushed her down.

Jackie hadn't meant to do anything wrong. She just didn't know any better. After meeting the insurance claim representative, he understood why.

He texted her. *Don't give back the money. Keep it. We have donated the stuff in my car to charity. Goodbye. I don't want to be with you anymore. Don't come down here again.*

He scrolled down to where he could block her. Staring at the blue, bold text. His mind told him to do it, but his heart still hoped that they could be friends someday.

The hotel room was paid up for three months. Pike decided to see what Jackie would do in those three months. If she straightened out, he would meet with her again. If she didn't, then it was over.

He raked his hand through his hair. No way was he going back to sleep. Pike grabbed a bottle of water from the fridge and turned on the news. His dad texted to say he was home. Pike called him quickly. "No issues on the roads?"

"Easy drive, son. Look, I've been thinking about this money. I'm going to put it into fixing up Wade's property."

Pike sat forward. "It's in the middle of nowhere."

"I know, but that place has meaning to me."

"Well, you own it. Do whatever you want with it."

"You do, son."

"I do what?"

"Own it."

"I own it?" Pike stood up. "I own his property? How can that be? I haven't paid anything on it. Is there a lot of back taxes? Geesh. Why didn't you tell me?"

"Wasn't the right time. I've been keeping up with the bills. How about considering that as your home base?"

"I don't know. I need to be near an airport, and that's . . . what . . . two hours from one?" Pike paced. "I like it here, dad."

"Well, think about it. He wanted you to continue his legacy."

"Driving? I am. I couldn't be closer to continuing. I am in the same job he was once."

"Just think about it."

"Why don't you move there?"

"Not giving up my life again."

"Was a family that bad?"

"No. No, Pike. You were a pain in the ass, but I was talking about something different. I left a lot on the table when I married your mother. I want it back."

"What?" Pike heard the bathroom door open. "Look, I have to go. I'll call you later."

"Good luck on your trip."

"Thanks." Pike hung up. Clair walked toward him with her hair wrapped up in a towel. "Sorry, did I wake you?"

"Want me to make you coffee?"

She dropped another bag by the door. "Yes, thanks."

Pike made her coffee, going through the motions. Was this how life was going to be? A platonic relationship? Roommates? She fired up her computer, typing with a glance here and there as the television announced the projected landfall of the Category 1 hurricane. Now all attention was on Georgia. "Hear from your dad yet?"

Pike brought over her coffee and placed it on the end table. "He's home."

"Are you okay?"

"I'm not going to get any help from him buying something down here."

She scrunched up her face. "Oh, poor baby. I'm so sorry daddy isn't buying you a house."

Pike turned. "I didn't mean it like that."

"Welcome to the club of making it on your own."

"He's putting the money into the family home. He wants me to settle in Virginia at my uncle's place. It's in the middle of nowhere."

That changed her attitude. "Are you?"

"I don't know what I'm going to do. I'll think it over on the road. Are you done in the bathroom?"

She took a sip from her mug. "All yours."

They arrived to a full hanger of jumpers. Pike texted 49 that they were here and sitting at their usual table.

Clair grinned through a mouthful of scrambled eggs. "You know, it's still a good idea you learn how to jump."

His eyes swept over the crowd. "I know. I asked 49 if the guys who he originally picked could come out. I like Miller and Nash."

"Hear from them since they left?"

"Nash sent me his congratulations."

"Out of that whole crew, I would never have guessed you two would hit it off. I can see Miller, but Nash? He's out there."

"How often do we partner with Colorado?"

"It used to be never. Now, with us driving specials, I am guessing a lot. Shit, hmm." Clair put down her fork and picked up her coffee.

"What?"

"Nothing."

"That's a pretty big nothing."

"I just realized we will be dealing with Colorado."

"You seem to deal with your brother okay."

"The other one."

Pike's heart wrenched up tight. She still had feelings for the guy who beat him up.

49 walked in, rubbing his hands. "It's a great day for a road trip, kids. Pike, grab a few bags of drinks and food. We need to fill the cooler. Big-size cooler. Waters, juices, fruit. Grab me some packaged pastries. I like the raspberry. Be right back."

Clair looked at Pike. "He's in a good mood."

Pike finished his last bite of egg. "Wonder what's up . . ."

He stopped speaking at the sound of men laughing from a table on the far side of the cafeteria. "Oh yeah, definitely bang her! She would be begging for more."

Pike snapped his head in the direction of the voices. Three guys were grinning as they gazed at Clair. Pike's skin chilled, his heart contorted, eyes stinging like they do with pine pollen in the air back in Massachusetts.

Clair touched his clenched fist and his stare darted to her hand resting on his. He realized she was saying something. "Pike? Pike?!" She was talking to him. "Dude? What's up?"

Clair leaned forward, but he pulled his fist back with such force that she retreated to her plate. "You're pale. Are you okay?"

He tapped his chest. "Heartburn." The men moved on to another topic.

49 sat down, coffee and doughnut in hand. Pike stood, gathering their food to go. 49 watched him. "He, okay?"

Clair tilted her head. "That was the strangest thing."

"What happened?"

"I don't even know how to explain it."

"Why don't you go help him. We are heading over to Cooper's in five."

Clair stood up, taking her tray. 49 insisted, "Pack pastries," making her grin.

Pike loaded a dozen bottles of water between two bags. Then, thinking it wasn't enough, he packed a dozen more. Clair caught up with him. "We are going to make stops."

"There's three of us. Just want to make sure we have enough for a few days." He took another bag, filling it with fruit, then another with granola and protein bars. "I'll go put these in the Jeep."

She offered, "Want some help?"

He tipped his head, throwing his chin to her. "I've got it. But I'm not packing that crap he eats, so this is your chance while I turn my back."

She chuckled, grabbing a bag for the muffins and pastries. 49 watched Pike walk past holding four bags in each hand, effortlessly. Some of the men sitting and eating took notice. Clair stopped at the table to show 49 what she grabbed for him and herself. He nodded and repeated he would be right out.

49 fixed another coffee to go, walking over to see if there was anything else he wanted for the trip. He was sure Pike had more fruit then the three of them would eat. He walked past and decided the two of them had packed what they needed.

49 pointed to the outdoor ice machine. "Grab us three bags. The water and juices have its own cooler."

Clair followed behind 49's Jeep as they drove into the hanger where the rig was being prepped. Pike grinned at the sight of the blue tires.

49 walked over to Captain Jacobowski, "Are we running on time?"

"On schedule." She unfolded her arms. "Kind of wish I was going with you."

49 asked Pike and Clair to unload all the stuff that was going in the rig. They made a pile as technicians transferred their cargo inside. Cooper walked from around the other side, clipboard in hand, flashing his light beneath the rig and marking up his paperwork.

Pike greeted Captain Jacobowski. She led him to a table where she had her own paperwork for him to sign.

Going over the packet, she explained each subfolder. His options for housing, meals, benefits. All things he could read while on the trip. She tucked it into a soft-cover briefcase and handed it over, shaking his hand.

Cooper invited Clair, Pike, and 49 into the rig. Clair took the driver's seat, with 49 riding shotgun and Pike squatting in the middle. A giant drop-down screen lowered from the ceiling, stopping right in front of the windshield. Cooper secured headphones with a mic attached. A light buzzing sounded inside the cab. All three of them glanced around as he adjusted the volume from a keyboard he was holding. "Testing, testing. Can you hear me clearly?"

Pike was amazed by the quality of the sound. "Dude, it sounds like you're in here with us."

Cooper nodded. "I was aiming for good quality."

"Achieved," said Clair

Cooper loaded the screen, displaying a picture of the inside of the cab. With a laser pointer, he singled out the first button. He then expanded a detailed picture below the full photo of the dash, enlarging each button and switch. They illuminated inside the cab, highlighting each button he referred to it.

When it came to the truck's design, Cooper had thought of everything. There was a satellite jammer, and the windshield was strong enough to withstand a rocket launcher. It was the next switch, however, that made Pike listen carefully.

Cooper installed retractable lightning rods on the cab and container. Pike liked this. He liked this a lot.

49 looked at the high-tech advances. "Pretty soon, they won't need drivers."

Cooper deadpanned, "I ran through scenario after scenario. I can't make a machine replicate the human brain's split-second decision-making. Humans are still needed."

He turned to find at the three of them staring at him. "Slide the cover to Row B, Number Eight, several inches to the right."

Pike found it first. A ten-inch hologram of Cooper appeared as if he were standing in front of the rig. All three of them looked on in fascination.

Pike tried to touch the hologram, only to block out part of the image's body. Pike then placed his hand below as if Cooper were standing in his palm. "Hey, look! I'm holding Cooper!" He grinned, amused with himself.

Clair batted his hand away while Pike carefully tried to rub the top of Cooper's head. Clair smacked him again. When the real Cooper turned around, so did the hologram. Pike prayed that he would say, "Help me, Obi-Wan Kenobi. You're my only hope."

Clair closed the panel. "Why do we have something like this? It's going to be a total distraction while we drive."

"You need me to be there if something goes wrong. Visual and 3D technology will keep you informed and thinking clearly. Also, in case you get bored while driving I have preprogrammed four hours of conversation."

Pike jolted forward. "So, we can have a debate? Like, I can debate with tiny Cooper?" Clair covered her face with her hands, knowing what was coming.

"Tiny Cooper?" asked Cooper.

Pike slid the cover back. "Yeah, this is mini-you." He gasped proudly, "Mini-Cooper!" He turned back to 49 like he was a genius. "Mini-Cooper! This is mini-Cooper!"

Mini-Cooper disappeared. Pike looked inside the slot. "Hey, where did you go?"

"Do not call me that. It's stupid and cliché."

Pike straightened up. "Sorry. Sorry, Coop."

They toured the cabin next. There was the third seat that could be pulled out from the side closet. It was affixed to a pole that locked in place with tracking in the floor. The back cab was fitted with two bunk beds. The top one folded into the wall and the bottom was stationary, with storage underneath. A television that could double for a computer monitor rested on one wall, with a window on the opposite side.

A cherry wood, full-length slim closet housed a small built-in refrigerator with microwave above. There was another door on the opposite wall that held a toilet, with a small sink to the side. This was home for the next few days. Pike dived on the bottom bed. "Cooper, you outdid yourself. Can I live in here? Please? Please?"

"There will be times you do. I had to consider that."

"You knocked it out of the park, buddy."

Clair interrupted them. Staring at her phone, she read the incoming text. "We are going to Colorado?"

Cooper's hologram appeared again. "Yes, how do you know?"

She dropped her phone to her side. "My brother is confirming the pickup point."

Pike glanced at Clair. "Escort? This is a test run?"

Cooper brought up a map on the screen. "Full escort there and back."

Captain Jacobowski climbed in as 49 maneuvered past them. She handed him the paperwork and he twirled his finger for her to go back out before he followed.

With everyone back on the pavement outside the rig, Clair stood, arms folded in front of her chest. "This is a one-day trip up and back. Colorado is not twenty-four hours. Not even one way."

Cooper agreed, "Technically you are right. It's twenty-five hours. Thus the escort run. We need to see if this rig can make it in under twenty-four hours."

"No cargo? Risky." Pike seemed skeptical.

Clair backed him. "You're asking for trouble on an empty container."

Cooper left the map up on the screen as he explained that they were coming back with a loaded trailer.

Knock Knock Knock... Who is it?

EIGHT HOURS UNTIL LAUNCH. The technicians left and it was just Cooper, Pike, Clair, and 49 waiting. Cooper decided to bring out his latest invention. The sky opened up with rain as Pike closed the hanger doors. "Maria must be early," he joked with Clair.

Cooper returned, shoulders slumped, muttering to himself. He handed them each a padded pouch. Pike pulled the Velcro free. Cooper pointed. "You can track the sky. Gives you an edge during the daylight."

Pike pulled out glasses that made him look like John Lennon. It took his vision a few moments to adjust to what he was actually

seeing. "What . . . ? What are these, Coop?"

Cooper slipped his own pair on. "Did you know bees can see the electromagnetic patterns in the sky?"

Pike walked a few unsteady steps, still adjusting his vision through the glasses. The blue tires were no longer powder blue. He could see other fibers woven in the rubber. He could see flecks of black that clung to the blue particles.

Pike extended his hand and focused. The graphing of his skin popped out. The dirt particles in between the folds of his skin, tiny dots attached to his arm hair. He shook his hand as if to free it from germs. "What the heck? Dude, what am I seeing?"

"Your early warning system. Don't scratch the glasses. Be super careful. It took me a year to perfect the magnetism and reflection into a single lens." He scolded Pike like a child, "I am completely serious. If they are not on your face put them back in the case."

Pike turned to Cooper. There was a shadow around his silhouette. "Dude, do I look like the irresponsible one? Coop, you have a dark cloud around you. Kind of a fog? It looks creepy."

"All humans do, but yours is light. Why is yours different?"

Clair and 49 fumbled to put their glasses on, staring at Pike and then Cooper. Clair admitted, "I see it."

49 stepped closer to Pike, "What in God's name?" Pike looked at his extended arms, then down his body. 'What? Light? I don't see anything?"

All at once a deafening snap shook the building and the ground beneath their feet, throwing everyone off-balance and diving for cover. Clair pushed herself up and shouted "EARTHQUAKE!" She removed her glasses and shoved them into the case as Cooper had instructed.

From the floor, Pike watched the air bend, reaching out his hand to touch the sharp points followed by smooth lines. He sat back onto his behind. He could see the movement of the air like pebbles disrupting a still pond.

Clair covered one ear with her hand and hunched her head to the side, trying to cover the other with her shoulder, all while helping 49 to his feet, pulling him toward the truck.

She motioned for Pike, then shouted at him to take cover. She gripped the new glasses tightly against her body, with 49 following close behind. Pike tilted his head back and watched the swirls of air at the top of the hanger. He suddenly realized this was the safest place to be, and they all scrambled under the semi, looking up to see if the roof was caving in.

They were safe beneath the solid frame of the semi's trailer, but not for long. They were in an open building, watching for any movement from the structure, crouched down, waiting. Pike squatted, glasses still on his face with the fingers on his left hand touching the pavement.

The air was still, but he felt the vibrations.

"Do you guys feel that?" All heads turned to stare at him.

"Feel what?" asked Clair.

"There's that hum again."

"Hum?"

"Like that time in the hanger. The floor. It's vibrating." He was looking down at the concrete.

Clair concentrated. "I don't feel anything."

Cooper disbelievingly shook his head. "No. No. No! No! We have seconds to make it inside that door." He looked wildly in all directions, then pointed toward a nearby door. "Run!"

All four of them sprinted as fast as they could. After waving them inside, Cooper secured the door with an odd ritual, then flipped a switch, illuminating every corner in the room.

The air was vibrating, making Pike nauseous. He removed his glasses. "What do you think is there? Why is this room lit like this?"

"They are after me."

Pike turned to Clair and 49. Clair asked, "Who?"

Cooper pointed up. "Them."

"Why?" asked Pike.

Cooper paced. "Because I know things."

All three asked at once, "What?"

Cooper stopped pacing. "I know they exist. I know they have been taking test subjects and I know they want me."

Clair stepped forward. "The disappearances?"

Pike tried to lighten the mood. "You are pretty spectacular, Coop. Who wouldn't want you?"

Clair smacked his arm. "Not the time."

Pike removed his glasses, holding them by the side. Clair took them and properly stored them the way Cooper requested.

Cooper watched the care she took with his invention. "Thank you." She nodded, not thinking anything of her act.

49 asked, "Why don't you have more security here?"

"Attention. Besides, I don't want anyone to get hurt. They can't get in. We are safe."

49 asked what was on all their minds, "For how long?"

"They don't like commotion. Exposure is the last thing they want."

"Why cover it up then?"

Cooper started to pace again. "Are you kidding me? The public would be insane knowing this stuff. Look, it's complicated. They want me. They can't have me. I am staying right here and continuing to learn what I can with every bit of evidence they leave behind."

Pike asked, "Is the truck okay out there?"

"Outside of this room, that is the next safest place you could be."

49 looked relieved and Clair nodded. "Good to know."

Pike asked with an uneasy feeling, "What could happen between here and Cheyanne Mountain and back? Don't skimp on the details."

Room to Grow

VALENTINE ARRIVED WITH a crew of four teammates. "Blue tires?"

Clair nodded and kept her arms folded. "Don't knock the tires. They're the least of our concerns this trip."

"Well, it's certainly going to bring on curiosity."

He walked the rig, approaching Pike from behind. "Evans." Pike turned as Valentine held out his hand. "Congratulations! You're official."

Pike's features lightened. "Thanks, man. Thanks for everything."

Valentine patted Pike's shoulder with his left hand. "You're a Double Negative now."

Pike grinned. "Probably been that my whole life." Valentine chuckled and let go of the handshake. "It's official now."

They walked around the rig. "Heard about your house back home. Glad no one was hurt."

"That's a story."

"Your girl down here?"

"We delivered her back. She was a suspect, but I think she got cleared."

"That's good."

"Let me ask you, do you have a girlfriend? Wife?"

"Wife."

"You're gone a lot. How does it affect home life?"

"Denise is a flight attendant. She schedules her days for when I'm working, so I might be the wrong person to ask."

"That is pretty convenient. She got any single friends?"

Valentine smirked. "There's always the lot lizards."

Pike frowned. "No thanks. Besides, how does that work with an escort team and a driving partner?"

Valentines laughed. "What about you and Morris?"

"What about what?"

"You two seem to hit it off. Never seen her so protective of anyone before."

"I think she still has feelings for her ex."

"Hanskon? That's over. Especially after his attack on you."

"I'm not so sure about that."

"Look, relax. Have you found a place to live yet?"

"I'm staying at Clair's until I decide."

"That's convenient."

"No, no. Not like that."

"Here is my advice. Move onto the base for a while. Lots of little honeys come through there for training. Maybe you will meet someone."

They reached Clair and the group. Pike nodded. "Good idea."

Clair turned, observing Valentine first and then Pike. "What's a good idea?"

"Evans getting housing on the base until he figures out where he wants to be."

Clair's face dropped. "Fine." She turned her back to Pike, her jaw shifting like the plates of an earthquake.

Captain Jacobowski hadn't noticed the mood shift. "Which one of you is driving first?"

Clair answered abruptly, "Evans," causing Pike to playfully roll his eyes at her.

She kept her arms folded and her jaw clenched, staring hard. He nodded, giving in. "That's fine."

She turned back as Valentine rested a hand on Pike's shoulder. "No worries on my watch. We're swapping you out in Kentucky."

Pike made sure the speed limit wouldn't be an issue this time out. "We need to make it to Cheyanne in less than twenty-four hours. Have you been briefed?"

"Yes. Stay tight and close. Trust me on our speed. We will get you there. Safe. You're traveling empty, right?"

"Light and dangerous."

"Gotcha covered."

Captain Jacobowski handed 49 a clipboard. "Gas up before you hit Kentucky."

Valentine stepped toward 49. "Which route are they sending us?"

49 took the second copy and handed it to Valentine. He nodded, noting the time. "Let's saddle up, people. Time to get these blue tires out in the public."

Cooper and Pike did the final check. Cooper had to wipe the perspiration from his forehead. Pike watched, concerned. "Are we going to be okay?"

Cooper knit his eyebrows close together. "Of course. Why?"

"Why? Because you don't look too confident."

"It's going to work. All of it."

"You sure?"

"Yes." Cooper stood up. "I will be on standby day and night."

"We'll be fine."

Cooper was serious. "It can take 40,000 amps."

Pike jerked his head back. "Excuse me?"

"The truck, the tires. It can withstand a direct hit. You will be safe. If you can't engage the rods in time, you will still be protected."

Pike stepped closer to Cooper. "Do you know something I don't?"

"I saw the footage."

"The lightning thing at the hanger?"

"Yes, plus this afternoon."

"Is there footage from this afternoon?"

"Yes."

Clair stepped closer. "I want to see it."

Pike nodded. "Me too."

Cooper looked around. "It was nothing, just a direct hit."

Clair demanded, "Show us."

Cooper pulled out his tablet and the big screen came to life. 49 and Captain Jacobowski stopped their conversation as everyone turned to look. Cooper tapped a few times. "Here it is." The camera went white as the bolt of lightning directly hit the rod. It was over in a second.

Captain Jacobowski command, "Keep playing the footage."

Cooper reluctantly hit play again as the five of them stepped closer to the screen. She pointed. "Take a look at what comes next."

The rod turned orange as a white string snaked upward toward the top and shot out, cascading eight tenacles that dropped and hugged the roof. Pike examined the movements. "Is it searching? Looks like its combing over this hanger?"

Cooper confirmed. "Not the first time. They can't get in."

Clair and Pike looked to the roof. Pike was stunned by Coopers matter-of-fact demeanor. "Dude, how many times?"

He shrugged. "A few."

"But you said we are safe, right?"

He nodded. "They want me, not you."

Pike held up his hands in alarm. "Whoa, whoa, whoa! Are you safe, buddy? Maybe you should come with us."

Clair nixed the invite. "He's safer here."

Cooper admitted, "I get carsick."

Clair confirmed, "Absolutely not coming with us."

Cooper shrugged. Pike glanced at the stack of skateboards. "Skateboarding doesn't bother you?"

"Different kind of motion. Low to the ground. Besides, it's the quickest way to get around in here."

Pike understood. "So it's a height thing?"

He shrugged again. "Possibly."

"Planes?"

"Won't fly now."

Clair interrupted Pike's research Q&A. "I'll do the safety check. It's almost time to head out."

49, Maggie, and Clair made their way toward the rig. Pike hung back with Cooper.

Cooper grabbed Pike's hand. "Something happened to you that night. When you get back, I want to try some more tests with you. Don't say anything to anyone."

"Nothing happened to me. I've had enough tests."

Cooper squeezed Pike's hand as hard as he could without getting any reaction from Pike. "See? You should feel that. Nothing. Not even a reaction."

Pike glanced down, easily removing his hand from Cooper's grip. "I need to get ready."

Pike turned and Cooper flung his hand out, landing hard on Pike's shoulder. "Karate chop!" He immediately retracted his hand and clutched it to his body, doubling over in pain.

Pike glanced over his shoulder. "You okay, buddy?"

Cooper shook his injured hand and said through gritted teeth, "See? Nothing."

Pike walked away as Cooper ran up and kicked the back of Pike's leg. Pike felt that, but only a little. Just enough to start getting annoyed. "Would you stop it?"

Cooper was jogging to keep up. "See? See? When you get back, we are running tests."

Pike raised his hand and kept walking without looking back. "Whatever, pal."

Clair, 49, and Pike went over last-minute details with Valentine. Clair barely made eye contact with Pike. They had to pack special hazmat suits that resembled the jumpsuits racecar drivers wear. They had blue and white stripes, the same color as the trailer.

The entire security detail had to wear them, causing the guys to mutter about how stupid they looked. Valentine pointed to a man named Ronaldo, insisting there was good reason for the extra layer. "Shut up and put the damn thing on." That shut him up.

Pike, Clair, and 49 only needed to wear them when they were outside of the cab. Everyone was on edge, but they were ready to do this. Pike climbed in, adjusting the driver's seat and station. He glanced over the panel. "Bet this thing can almost drive itself."

49 opened the door to slide the third seat out. Pike climbed off his seat to help. It was pretty straightforward to assemble. The chair unfolded with locking pins to keep it in position. Cooper even gave it its own safety harness. 49 let it hang. No way was he getting himself tangled in that.

Pike returned to his seat. An incoming text from Jackie appeared on his phone as it started to link to the Bluetooth system. The text flashed up on the windshield. *Pike I am going to get a job up here. Put money away for us. I want to only be with you.*

He grabbed his phone, trying to shut down the sync. Clair and 49 had already read the text. "See, she's a changed woman. You two are perfect for each other."

He flipped his phone over. He didn't dare text back. Clair, offered not wanting to see the Jackie saga light up the windshield any further, "Would you like me to get that off of the Bluetooth?"

He handed Clair his phone. "Please."

She tapped at the screen a few times and then handed it back. "Good, now you can keep Jackie to yourself."

Clair picked up her phone and did some texting of her own. It annoyed Pike, making him miss his check-in signal over the talkie. He was not going to let Clair get to him. She was pissed off for no reason and taking it out on him. Whatever her problem was, it was hers and hers alone. Not his.

49 observed the two of them. He guided Pike to answer Valentine. Cooper's hologram appeared. "Let's get her out and introduce her to the roads."

Pike started the rig. The engine roared to life. An adrenaline rush surged through Pike, making him twitch. He redirected the energy, rubbing his hands together. "This is dope. Ready to test this bitch, tiny Cooper?"

Cooper reminded him of the sequence of switches to flip for lights. The rig illuminated, making Pike feel like a badass behind the wheel. The engine hummed and Clair answered Valentine on Pike's behalf. "I think he just ejaculated."

Pike snapped his head to the side. "Excuse me?"

She handed Pike the talkie. "He's been waiting for you to answer."

Pike took the mic. "Sorry about that. In the moment and not familiar with protocol yet."

"Let rock and roll, Agent 50399"

"Copy that."

Slow and Slower

THERE WERE BENEFITS to driving slowly. Pike watched the reactions on people's faces when they saw the blue tires. He laughed at kids with jaws dropped open or ear-to-ear grins. Clair kept checking her mirror to see if the asphalt was making its mark on them yet. Nothing that she could detect. "Cooper, why aren't the tires marked up yet?"

"Formula. I told you, I perfected it, Agent Morris."

"Yeah, but there is oil in the asphalt. You don't have control over that."

"Agent Evans, how does she handle?"

"Like a dream, Cooper. Smooth and comfortable. You nailed it. I could drive this baby all day, every damn day."

"Good."

"Do we have tunes in here?"

Cooper typed something into his keyboard as 49 looked up and around as AC/DC's "Highway to Hell" kicked the speakers to life. Pike grinned. "Hell yah!"

Out on the open highway, Valentine made good on his promise to bump up the speed. They had eight hours to reach the destination and now was his time to make up for their previously slow and steady pace.

Exactly eight hours later they were pulling into the exchange site. A team of three black Suburbans waited. Valentine exchanged greetings with the team leader and instructed them about the jumpsuits.

Clair, Pike, and 49 suited up then got out to stretch and fill the fuel tank. When Pike and Clair did the truck inspection, Valentine brought Billy Johnson over for introductions. He checked out the rig, whistling his appreciation of the clean lines and how she would light up the middle of the night. Most of his comments were saved for the blue tires.

He finally got down to business, handing 49 the new papers and asking which one of them was driving. Clair stepped forward. "My run."

He eyed her, trying to size her up. He hesitated, glancing from Pike to 49. Pike offered, "I wouldn't underestimate this one. It will be your biggest mistake. Dude . . . just saying."

He conceded, removing the toothpick from his mouth. "Well, all right, folks. Hope you know how to move this rig. We will keep in a tight formation. I will use the lights."

Pike cocked his head. "Headlights?"

"Wagers and blues. We are meeting the Yetis in Junction City, Kansas. Now it says here nine-point-five hours. We will be shaving a considerable amount of time off, so keep up sweetheart."

Pike protested. "What? Why does she get to have all the fun?"

"I can keep up just fine. So, you are aware, the load is empty."

Valentine shook Pike's hand. "Watch out for Billy. If Morris seems stressed, speak up."

"She will be fine." Pike glanced around. "Might grab a few winks. Looks like I will be doing the last leg of our journey."

"See you back here in a few days. Stay alert around the Yetis."

Pike shrugged. "Fuck 'em. Now I know their game."

"Remember, we are all on the same team."

"My mother is Scottish. The past is never the past. We only remember our grudges."

"Well, then there is nothing left to say about that."

Pike bobbed his head. "Have you noticed Clair can flip like a switch?"

"Morris? No, why?"

"This morning she was nice. But the whole ride down she has been snapping at me."

Valentine laughed. "Another reason to get your own place."

"I'll talk to 49 about it."

Valentine smirked. "It's funny you call Kittrick that."

"It's all I could remember when we met. It stuck."

Valentine patted Pike's upper arm. "Call me if you need anything."

Pike's thoughts screamed; *I need you to drive faster*. But he smiled. "Thanks, man."

He rejoined his group and reminded Johnson that Cooper wanted all the guys to wear the jumpsuits. He gestured to his men. "Hey, suit up or perish." They laughed, waving him off. All but two of them changed into jumpsuits.

Pike walked to the passenger side and sat in back, securing the third seat that 49 had occupied. 49 climbed in. "You are in my seat."

Pike grinned. "Thought I'd give you the better view."

"The view doesn't change much after four decades. Unless you plan on resting before the next swap?"

"That is exactly what I am planning to do."

"Okay, kid. Stay where you are then."

Pike gave 49 a thumbs up.

Clair climbed in, adjusted the seat, and checked in with Johnson. She then handed Pike his phone. No messages. She felt better about that.

49 handed over Clair's phone and she placed it in the cupholder where Pike had set his. He looked at his phone and placed it in his sweatshirt pocket. Pike asked, "Anyone need a water?"

Clair raised a finger. "I'll take one."

49 checked the time. "I suppose I have to wash my pills down with something."

Pike walked to the back and grabbed a few from the cooler. Johnson called over the talkie that they were moving out and once they were back on the highway they were motoring.

Cooper appeared as his hologram. "This is what I was talking about. I can track you everywhere."

Clair argued. "You and how many others?"

"I can also jam signals from outside the rig."

Pike grinned. "Did you check the web to see if anyone posted the truck with blue tires?"

"All photos have been wiped."

"You know, Coop. Maybe you could put a positive spin on this. Make another one of these and have it visit disaster sites loaded with water and supplies, or like one of those trucks that people can do their laundry at?"

"Interesting idea. I suppose I could make a few replicas without the technology you are carrying."

"Or at least stick blue tires on some of the existing trucks?"

"Not sure I could use it for FEMA transports, but this gives me another idea. I'll put some thought into it. Good suggestion."

They reached the highway, and Johnson wasn't kidding. Lights flashed and wagers blinked as the speedometer climbed. They were passing everything. Clair kept up tight and uncomfortably mentioned, "I don't mind eighty, but ninety is asking for trouble. I don't like this, Kittrick. Does he know I have no weight in the back? I can't stop this suddenly."

49 nodded. "Agreed. But I think the only thing you have to worry about is other trucks and animals this time of night." He picked up the talkie. "Johnson, Agent 49637. This rig doesn't have the stopping power for the current speed in emergency situations. Let's scale back some."

Pike leaned, forward checking the side mirrors. "What's this guy thinking? It's truckers in commuter traffic."

Johnson backed off to eighty without answering them.

Within two hours the road widened and the tractor trailer traffic thinned. Johnson brought the speed back up, with Clair still uncomfortable hauling at this pace. "I'm all for getting there cutting the time, but this guy is crazy."

Pike was sleeping in the back as 49 observed the night sky. "Stick with it. Good training for our urgent runs."

"Urgent runs?"

"No one is in any danger unless a tire blows."

Cooper's hologram appeared. "These tires can withstand heat and wear in excessive circumstances. This is nowhere near an excessive circumstance. The speed is not an issue, Morris. She can handle it."

"Neumann, you hear our conversations?"

"Yes, 24/7. I need to know immediately if there is an issue. As I said, the speed is no issue for the tractor or trailer. Turn on the commuter screen."

Clair looked over all the switches. Her eyes concentrated for too long on the instruments and the rig drifted to the right. Agent Johnson's voice awakened the talkie. "Is there a problem, agent?"

She grabbed the talkie. "No. Too many buttons and gadgets in this new rig. It won't happen again."

"Copy that."

49 reached out. "Pay attention to the road, I've got it. Neumann, which switch?"

Cooper instructed 49 as a grid filled the windshield. Clair's mouth dropped open. "What the hell?"

It placed every vehicle on the road within a half mile ahead and a quarter mile behind. It clocked each speed showing the MPH number on each car. Heat dots appeared in each one to reveal the number of occupants and where they were seated. Weapons were identified. All three armored vehicles showed a list of what they were carrying, the make and model information sat next to a picture of each vehicle.

Each vehicle was displayed on the grid. If one swayed out of its lane or came too close to the center divider its display color switched to red and stayed that way until it was completely in the new designated lane. One vehicle listed a handgun in the glove compartment. No concern to them.

"Cooper Neumann, you are a genius. This is incredible." Clair instantly felt safer about her speed. "Wait until Evans sees this."

After five hours of sleep, Pike awoke to darkness. They were two hours away from the exchange where the Yetis were picking them up. Pike made his way to the front and exchanged seats with 49, who grabbed the bed for a nap.

There was only their convoy on the road. Johnson was still traveling with his flashers on. Pike scrubbed his face with his hands. "Isn't that driving you nuts?"

Clair grinned. "Used to it, I guess. Hey, check this out." She flipped the switch that showed the map of vehicles on the road. It now displayed the nighttime version of the screen.

Pike leaned in. "No way! This is dope."

Cooper appeared as his hologram, making Pike jump. "Jesus, Coop. You scared me."

"Sorry. I also programed in weather patterns. Touch the lower-right corner of the windshield."

"The windshield is a touchscreen?"

"You brought this back from Ohio."

"Sweet!" Pike touched it, studying the graphs and layout. Then he saw a line zipping its way closer from behind. "Hey, Coop? What is that?"

Cooper's hologram showed that he was working at a touchscreen himself. "Not quite sure. The air to surface area is equalized."

Pike tilted his head, leaning forward to observe the sky through the windshield then, then turned and looked out the passenger side. "I don't see any cloud coverage."

"There is a weather disturbance thirty miles behind you."

A lightning bolt ripped through the sky above and faded off miles in front. Pike shifted to Clair. "Or maybe it's Thor."

She grinned. "I am team Loki."

Pike sat back. The screen was clear. "Really? I figured with Hanskon practically being Thor's twin that you were into that type."

She didn't need his wisecracking shit right now. She was tired. Tired and now pissed off. "Better Thor than that little piece of white trash you keep rescuing from the shelter. At least Jon has a job."

Cooper's hologram disappeared. Pike glanced back to where 49 was sleeping. He lowered his voice to a loud whisper. "She doesn't throw sucker punches or plan sneak attacks. At least she shows her emotions right up front."

Clair clenched her jaw, trying to be as quiet as she could to let 49 rest. "You're right. The world just revolves around her, and she throws little childish temper tantrums when she doesn't get her way. But I guess that's what you're into. Needy, immature girls."

"She doesn't have anything. Her mother was a drug addict and abandoned her when she was little. She was raised in foster homes. I agree that she is manipulative and selfish but it's what she learned to survive."

"Look, Evans, here's the thing. I don't care. You do what you want. You're moving out. I don't have to see it or listen to it. But you know what, even you can't ignore the fact that you're miserable around her. She sucks the life out of you. When she was around you were grumpy and on edge. The minute we left her behind you became fun again."

Pike wanted to say something. He opened his mouth and scrunched down his eyebrows. Not sure how to answer, he decided to stay quiet. Another lightning bolt zipped by. They both glanced up to watch. A moment passed with neither one saying anything.

Pike sighed. "I like Loki."

Clair watched the road. They were the only ones on this stretch of highway. Pike changed the screen back to the vehicle grid. "How are you holding up?"

"I'm getting tired."

Pike offered, "Want me to ask them to pull over so we can switch?"

She held her hand up. "I'm good. I will finish." She glanced back over at him. "Thanks, though."

Pike nodded. "Who's taking us in from the Yetis?"

"Team One."

"I don't know who that is."

"Yes, you do. The ones who handed you your ass."

"Seriously?"

"Eli, Miller, Nash, Martinez, Alfie. You will recognize the others. We have them both directions. In and back out."

"Your boyfriend gonna be there?"

"Not sure."

Pike glanced around. "Man, there is nothing out here."

The *crack* and a blinding white flash hit at the same time. Clair jammed the breaks as she and Pike shielded their eyes from the burst of light. The rear escort swerved into the median. 49 leapt out of the bed, grabbing onto the side rail.

The flash disappeared in an instant. A moment later, Cooper's hologram appeared and the truck finally came under control, with Johnson's voice shouting over the talkie.

Clair scrambled to find the talkie, still blinking sight back into her eyes. "Here. We're okay." The scent of lavender played in the air.

The headlights illuminated a streak of steam as it wafted away. Johnson's team pulled over to the right in the breakdown lane. Headlights were pointed in every direction.

Clair stopped the truck at an angle, taking up both lanes. "I have to move." She called over the talkie, shaking as she straightened the rig, driving into the breakdown lane ahead of Johnson's vehicle.

Johnson ordered her to stay where she was. He called out over the talkie for the rear escort team, but got no response. He turned his truck around and drove in the oncoming line, assessing the damage.

Spots started to fade as Pike's eyesight returned. Cooper rattled off the gigajoules registering from the truck's diagnostics. 49 held onto the bars as he made his way toward the front. "What in God's name?"

Pike was wide-eyed. "I think we got hit by lightning." He could smell the lavender more strongly now.

Clair responded, "I think the ground under us was hit." She wrinkled up her nose. "Do you guys smell . . . lavender?" 49 inhaled and Pike nodded. "I thought that was just me."

Cooper chimed in. "Correct, you do smell lavender. I installed aromatherapy into the ventilation system. The truck did not take a direct hit."

Pike breathed deeply, pleased with the scent. "That's dope. What other scents are in here?"

Shouting from the talkie cut short the conversation. It was from the rear escort team. "Ronaldo is missing. Repeat. Ronaldo is missing!"

49 pulled out his phone. "I'm calling this in. We're sitting ducks out here."

Clair picked up the talkie. "Agent 50287 to base."

A female voice answered, "Go ahead, Agent 50287."

"There is a situation. Requesting air team."

49 interjected, "Exchange point needs a double escort."

Clair repeated the request. Air security was in route and a specialty team would be deployed. The Yetis were closer than Johnson's second ground team.

Johnson's voice came over the talkie, confirming both their vehicles were operational.

Three air teams were deployed. The highway was contained and sealed. State and local police assisted.

Pike was still curious about the aromatherapy, and he asked Cooper if that was something they could control from inside the cab. Clair left the driver's seat to use the bathroom. They sat there for another ten minutes waiting for the go-ahead.

Two of the air squads had finished searching the grounds. It was time to get out of there. The airships hovered low, escorting Johnson's lead team, with Clair still behind the wheel of Pike's truck.

The Yetis arrived early, intercepting the trucks a good forty minutes closer than the original drop exchange. One air crew departed. Eli jockeyed to the front of the convoy, with Johnson and two vehicles following to the fuel stop. Cooper complained about a jammed signal under the truck. All the Yetis were already suited up.

Eli confirmed convoy's ETA when they were ten minutes out, as did both vehicles behind along with the air crew. 49 walked to the back of the cabin, now on the phone with Captain Jacobowski.

Clair tried to sound calm. "Will you go with me to drop off the paperwork?"

"Yeah, sure." Pike turned his head slightly to look at her. "I get why there's a strain between you two."

"What?"

"You and Eli."

"What does that have to do with anything?"

"Oh, I thought that's why you want me there."

"Fuck no! I don't give two shits about him. I'm asking in case I miss a detail when I explain this. We have to fill out a report."

"Oh."

"I usually carry a recorder, but I took it out of my bag this morning. It's next to my computer."

"Eli seemed pissed about the early intercept."

Clair furrowed her eyebrows. "Shut up. Stay out of it."

"I'm not saying this to butt in. Just the way he disrespects your dad and doesn't give you any credit. It almost looked like he was blaming you for what just happened."

"Evans, I don't have time to unpack all the bullshit with my brother. I don't care what he thinks one way or the other."

"I'm kind of lucky that way, I guess. Don't have any siblings."

"Clearly."

Pike was annoyed. "What is that supposed to mean?"

"You act like an only child."

"What's the difference?"

"You haven't learned when to shut up."

Pike jabbed his finger in the air. "That has nothing to do with being an only child. It's my mother's fault. She taught me to argue."

"She taught you to selectively argue. You suck at handling Jackie."

Pike looked away. "You're right about that."

Cooper's hologram reappeared. "I am still getting a disruption from the driver's-side receivers."

Clair shifted her eyes from the hologram to Pike. He was sitting back against the headrest, letting his shoulders relax. She answered, "We will check it when we fuel."

Pike agreed. "Could the lightning strike have blown something?"

"No. Program this number in." Cooper displayed a phone number through his hologram.

Pike followed his instructions. "Got it, buddy. I'll call you when we stop, and you can tell me where to check. But we have to fill out a quick report first."

Cooper acknowledged. "I'll be waiting."

Family Ties, Strong Binds.

THEY PULLED IN. CLAIR went straight to Johnson, with Pike following. 49 stayed with the rig, stretching and walking around the trailer as Nash and Miller approached.

Johnson remained concerned about his missing teammate and put a call in to his guy back at the highway for an update. Jackson, Morris, and Evans waited to hear. Nothing yet. No sign of him.

Eli signed off the paperwork from Johnson, going over the final route and destination. Johnson was staying on for the next one hundred miles to meet Yeti Team Three, the group that escorted Clair and Pike a few weeks ago to this same destination. Colorado Springs, the Cheyenne Mountain Complex.

From the fuel stop it was an estimated fifteen-hour

turnaround. Johnson agreed he would be here himself, waiting with fresh backup, and requested more of the jumpsuits.

Pike started to head back to the rig while Clair went inside the truck stop. Jackson followed Pike, asking about the rig. "Outside of what happened earlier, how does she ride?"

Pike grinned. "Like a dream. Cooper outdid himself."

Jackson nodded and awkwardly offered, "Congratulations."

Pike lifted an eyebrow. "Thanks?"

"Look, as much as I don't like you, we are on the same team."

"I suppose if I were just some random recruit you would have a different opinion of me."

"Exactly. Glad you understand."

"I don't. That makes no sense. Which leads me to believe you just don't like your sister."

"This isn't the line of work she should be doing."

Pike spoke up. "I disagree. This is exactly what she should be doing. Too bad you're too dumb to see that. She's an excellent driver."

Jackson adjusted his stance. "Did you just call me stupid?"

Pike raised his hand and shook a finger in the air. "I said you were dumb, not stupid."

Then he remembered Cooper wanted him to check something. "Excuse me." He walked away from Eli and called Cooper.

Pike joined 49 as Cooper instructed him where to look. Pike squatted down. "I don't see anything, dude. Wait, let me turn on the flashlight on my phone."

49 interrupted, pulling a travel-size flashlight from his pocket. "Pike, here."

Pike reached for the flashlight, grinning, "Thanks, dad."

49 smirked as Pike ducked under the truck again, turning on the flashlight. He saw what looked like tattered material. "There's something. Hang on." He slid deeper under the trailer. "You could have made more room under here. Jesus, it's tight."

He moved his body in a better position. He could see white material with torn strands hanging from it. "What the heck?" Pike moved the flashlight and angled his head to get a better view.

He leaned in just a little more before his eyes sprung wide and he screamed. He jerked his head back, slamming it against the underside of the trailer, causing him to drop his phone and the flashlight. "Ah! What the fuck?!?"

Scrambling backward, he scraped his shoulders against more of the truck's metal as he frantically tried to free himself.

"There's a body! There is a fucking burned body in there!" Pike ran to a nearby trash barrel, dry heaving into it.

49 shouted, "Jackson!" Nash, Miller, Johnson, and Eli ran toward 49, catching sight of Pike heaving over the barrel. "What the hell?"

Pike pointed toward the truck. "Dead body! Dead body!" He coughed and spit.

Jackson ducked under the rig, with Miller and Alfie at his heels. He picked up the flashlight and Pike's phone. Cooper was still yelling into it, "What?! Pike? What is it?"

Jackson confirmed. "Call it in. Looks like we found the missing guy." Cooper was shouting through the phone. Jackson grimly informed him that they'd found the top half of a man jammed up under the trailer.

Clair walked toward the crowd. Nash stood with Pike, looking pale and worried. "What's going on?" she asked.

It looked like all the blood had drained from Pike's face. He pointed. "Dead body stuffed up in there. Cooper asked me to check. I crawled under. Dead fucking body. There is a dead body."

Jackson crawled out from under the truck, still talking on the phone. Clair waited, walking to stand next to 49. "Really?"

"Apparently we found the missing guy."

"I don't understand. How?"

49 kept his eyes fixed on Pike while he asked Nash, "He okay?"

"He'll be fine."

Jackson hung up and gave Pike's phone to 49. "Get comfortable. We're going to be here for at least a few hours. The medical examiner is on his way. Neumann says the event registered about two hours ago."

Jackson watched as Nash tried to calm Pike down. "Don't suppose there was some random guy walking on the highway who stepped in front of you?"

Clair scowled. "Never that easy, is it?"

"Then I guess we know who it is."

Federal agents had the fuel stop sealed off before the locals even knew there was an incident. The body was extracted as Yeti Team Three arrived. Now there were six armored vehicles to escort their rig in.

Johnson muttered to himself, "What the fuck was that? I mean, it was just lightning?"

The crews had begun fighting over the rig. The specialty unit wanted to take it in for inspection, but 49 refused to budge. After several phone calls and even more agents arriving, Yeti team One and Three were granted clearance to escort the rig to its destination.

Pike was the driver, with Clair in the jump seat, too awake to sleep, and 49 in the passenger seat, keeping an eye on Pike after the day's events.

Pike could still smell a hint of lavender hanging in the air. "I like this scent."

For once, Jackson and Johnson agreed on the best course of action. They would arrive as quickly as possible. At an hour and fifteen minutes out from their departure, Johnson broke off from the convoy and headed back. They were five and a half hours away from their destination.

Clair finally hit the wall, blaming the scent of lavender, and made her way back to grab some sleep. Each hour, a few streaks of lightning cut across the sky. It made Pike think they were being followed. Maybe he was being paranoid. Maybe it was simply storms in the distance.

"Do you think that is part of our bolt friend?" 49 watched the sky. "Right now, I don't know what to think. Never in all my years has anything like this happened."

He glanced over to Pike. "Other humans were always the biggest threat. I don't have a clue about this shit."

Pike turned to look at 49, then shifted his eyes back to the road. "Do you think they're aliens?"

"I was never paid to think. I was paid to drive."

Pike leaned forward and searched the sky. "They seem to be heading in the same direction as us."

"Great."

Pike looked down to where Cooper's hologram should display. "Hey, Cooper? You awake?"

The hologram appeared. "Yes."

"What are we picking up?"

"A final part."

"For what?"

"Advanced technology I am working on."

"Can you see the lightning? It seems to be heading in the same direction as us."

"I am monitoring it. The air around you is stable. I will let you know if it changes."

"Appreciate that, dude."

49 was still concerned about Pike. "You handled that well."

"We lost a man."

"I have been lucky in my career. The only thing that has gone missing was cargo."

"I mean, did the guy have family? Kids? Oh, geez, I hope he doesn't have kids."

"Most of the agents are single. This is a high-risk division. I should have been clearer about that with you."

Pike jerked his head in 49's direction. "Hey, I know the risks. I get it." He turned back to the road. "I'm not worried about me. It's you, Clair, Nash, Cory, LaRue, and Valentine I worry about. You guys are like my family now."

"I hear you, kid."

"Can we fight lightning?"

"Cooper and his team are working on new technology."

Pike grinned sarcastically. "More training?"

49 nodded, then inhaled slow and deep. "More training."

Pike took notice. "How do you feel?"

"Me? Like a new man. Should have had that pacemaker put in years ago when they first suggested it."

Pike was relieved to see 49 was recovering nicely. "That's good news. Heart surgery has come a long way."

"Maybe that's why I waited."

"Hey, Cooper?"

Cooper's hologram appeared. "I don't see any activity."

"Oh, um . . . sorry. I just wanted to know more about this aroma thing you installed. I liked the lavender, but do you have anything that might keep me more alert?"

"Yes."

Pike waited a moment. Both he and 49 sniffed the air at the same time. Pike wondered aloud, "Mint?"

"Smells like mint."

"Is that mint, Coop?"

"Peppermint."

"Does peppermint keep you alert?"

49 shrugged.

They cruised along between 85 and 90 mph, just like before, eager to arrive as quickly as possible. No flashing lights were needed at this hour.

After a while, 49 showed Pike how to set the windshield as a travel grid that displayed the traffic around them, showing other truckers ahead in the distance. "At least we have other trucks now. Gives me something else to pay attention to."

Pike nodded. "Same." He sat back. "I do like that we're partnered."

49 nodded. "It's a good and bad distraction. Night is good. Daytime, you wish you were the only one on the road."

"True."

"Tell me, kid, are you okay after seeing that?"

"I think so. I just didn't expect a burnt torso stuffed up in there. Was that the guy who didn't have his jumpsuit on? I didn't see anything that looked like these jumpsuits." Pike glanced down. "I'm also grateful I didn't actually meet him. That would have been worse."

"I want to make sure you're okay."

"Thanks. I appreciate it."

They caught up to other truckers. Their blue tires stuck out like a sore thumb, with comments flying all over the radio. One trucker voiced his disbelief, arguing maybe it was just time to pull over and get some sleep. Another affirmed he would never do drugs again after seeing blue wheels on the road.

Pike listened to the CB chatter. "Hey Coop, your tires are a hit." No response. Pike shrugged and smiled at 49.

Another streak of lightning zipped through the sky. This one came in lower than the others. Both Pike and 49 looked upward. Pike picked up the talkie. "I don't like what I just saw. Can the guys behind me move to the front? The trailer is empty and the attack was on the guarding vehicle behind us."

Jackson's voice came over the receiver. "Yeti Three, move to the front."

Pike exhaled nervously. "I'm glad he listened. Damn it, I forgot to grab some water."

"Hang tight, kid, I'll get it."

"Can you grab me some fruit while you're back there?"

"Got it." 49 watched as Clair slept. She was out cold after having been awake for at least the twenty-four hours, the way he figured it.

49 picked out a variety of fruit and grabbed the pastry bag for himself. Everything had a place. There was even a bag to put trash in. Cooper had really thought this through.

"Here you go, kid."

Commuter traffic had gotten underway. Pike tested out the daytime version of the traffic grid on the windshield. It illuminated in the same red color and was surprisingly just as clear as the night version.

Pike could pick out Eli's truck. It carried twice as much weapons as the others. Three hours to their destination. Traffic was getting thicker and Pike suddenly felt a sense of unease. He glanced toward 49. "How are you doing?"

49 adjusted in his seat. "Holding up just fine. How about you?"

"Not sure . . .. Hey, Cooper, you there?"

Cooper appeared. "There is a disturbance in the airwaves. Put on your glasses."

"I can't, I'm driving."

"Agent Kittrick, put on your glasses and tell me what you see."

49 slid his glasses on. "These crazy things . . . I don't know what I'm looking for."

"Look up. Tell me what you see."

49 leaned his head against the passenger-side window, looking up. "Swirls? Swirls. Is that the right answer?"

"Pike, there is a disturbance in the sky. Weather is clear and there are no tornados in the forecast."

"Coop, what does that mean?" Pike jammed the brakes as a body landed on his hood. He veered wildly and fought to get the rig back under control.

Jackson shouted over the talkie, "Report!"

Pike weaved through traffic, trying to not to hit his own escorts.

"A fucking body just fell out of the sky! It's on my hood."

A whipping blur of golden-blonde hair waved like a flag as the head lifted up off the hood. A bloody head. Pike watched, unable to pull the rig off to the side, as the woman on the hood pushed herself slowly upward.

The upper-torso lifted and there she was, looking straight into the windshield. Pike slammed the breaks harder, somehow staying on the road.

It was Jackie. He screamed, "WHAT THE FUCK?!" Clair raced to the front of the cab but saw nothing. She watched Pike gain control while 49 shouted into the talkie, "It's gone! Vanished!"

Pike straightened the rig out as the nearby traffic gave him plenty of room.

Clair didn't understand. "What happened?!"

Pike gasped. "Jackie. Dropped out of nowhere. Landed on the hood."

Cooper's hologram reappeared. "Something is going on. It's not over."

Clair leaned forward and examined the hood. "It's clean. No dents. A falling body would have dented it."

Then like torrential rain, Jackie after Jackie fell from the sky, splatting onto the road, the nearby cars, and the escort Suburbans.

Pike weaved wildly from side to side as he tried to avoid running them over.

Clair's mouth dropped open. "What the fuck?! Pull over! Pull over!"

Pike found a hole in the traffic and the entire team pulled over, surrounding his rig. Vonn's voice came through over the talkie, "Something wicked this way comes."

They sat in silence. Pike grabbed the glasses and looked up to the sky. The swirls were beating like a heart. One by one, the Jackie's disappeared, leaving no trace of their presence. Gradually, the swirls smoothed into tranquility, leaving only a mess of cars scattered on the highway.

49 grabbed the talkie. "Can't believe I'm doing this again." He pressed the side button. "Agent 4-9 . . ." before he could call in his number a dispatch agent stopped him. "Radio silence, agent. Cleanup

is en route. Birds are arriving for escort in thirty seconds plus or minus, or not at all."

Thirty seconds plus or minus. Pike remembered that saying from when he delivered helicopters in the Army. That was the 160th SOAR.

Pike marked the time. Twenty-five seconds. "Get ready, twenty seconds." Silence. At ten seconds, the sound of the helicopters reached them. *Whup whup whup, whup whup whup.* The birds were in sight. Jackson gave the order, "Move it out! Stay tight."

Clair hit Pike's arm. "Swap out."

They quickly switched seats. Pike walked straight to the back of the cab, closed the bathroom door, and puked.

Twenty minutes out from the destination the birds signed out and cut to the right. Pike sat himself in the jump seat. 49 turned and handed him a water bottle.

Pike reached for it. "Thanks, man."

Clair listened to her brother's orders, telling them which gate they were going to. Pike watched a camo Humvee drive past on Clair's side.

She glanced out the window. "Shit."

Pike asked, "You, okay?"

She turned back, giving him a slight, sarcastic grin. "You're not the only one who's seeing exes today."

Hanskon had arrived.

I'll Cut a Bitch

THEY WERE IN THE TUNNEL. Six escorts, Hanskon and Clair parked where they were flagged in. Everyone exited their vehicles, with Hanskon immediately laughing at their jumpsuits. No one was amused.

Apparently, they had all experienced the events on the highway the same as Pike. They just didn't know who the girl was that had been raining down on them. Pike didn't say. Neither did 49 or Clair.

Nash walked over to them. "That was a first. Never had blondes rain down like that, not even in my acid days."

Jackson approached Clair's group. "Good driving, both of you. Evans, I don't know how you avoided jackknifing that rig. Good job. We tried taking photos of the chicks raining down, but nothing processed on any of the phones. Is that rig equipped with cameras?"

Clair pointed toward the door. "Ask Cooper."

He shifted. "How?"

She was as much of a wreck as Pike. "Call his name. He appears as a hologram."

Nash nudged Jackson's arm. "I gotta see this." He followed Eli to the cab.

After five minutes they returned and Hanskon walked over. "Heard it was raining blondes? Brunettes are much more fun."

Clair excused herself, shoving past Hanskon. Pike asked 49, "This place have a bathroom or anything?"

"Come on, kid, I'll show you."

Hanskon grinned, looking up at Eli. "Well?"

"Freakiest thing I've ever seen. Chicks fell from the sky. I am sure there are going to be a lot of messed up people who got caught in the middle of that mess."

"They were just dropping from the sky?"

Nash nodded. "Yeah. Then they disappeared when the hit the vehicles or ground. Absolutely insane."

Jackson looked over to the doors Clair and Pike had gone through, admitting, "That damn kid steered out of several potential disasters. I thought for sure he was going to roll it."

A request for Jackson to report to the conference room came over a speaker built into the wall. Hanskon followed. The guards only allowed Eli to enter. Clair and Pike walked toward them and were allowed to pass.

49 stood outside with Hanskon, who quipped, "No worries, old man. I brought the big toys. You guys will be safe on your return."

"In your hands, that doesn't mean a whole lot."

Hanskon lost his toothy grin. "Noted." He glared down at 49 and strode past.

Three scientists wearing matching white lab coats asked question after question to the trio. As soon as he mentioned the incident on the plane they singled out Pike and asked him to follow them. He didn't want to go.

Clair insisted she be allowed to join him. Jackson tried to insist as well, but was denied. Clair was allowed to follow because she had seen Pike's experiences firsthand.

They were led to a sterile operating room. There was a small metal cage on a slab. Inside was what Pike recognized as one of the "marching ants" from before. Stepping closer, Pike could feel its energy. It turned from green to white to blue, changing with every step he took.

It hummed louder, causing the cage to vibrate. *Zut, Zut! Zut, Zut!*

Pike felt suddenly happy inside, yet he didn't know why. His body was warm. His emotions relaxed as though dopamine was washing through him. Clair stayed on guard and stopped Pike about seven feet from the cage.

The scientists were speaking, but Pike didn't hear a word, instead watching the contents of the cage. *Is this the little guy from the plane? How did he end up in here?* Warmth continued to flow through him. It was his little pal, Volt! Volt flattened out, extending beyond its cage and then back in.

Clair looked alarmed. "Is that thing safe?"

Pike stepped closer, a wide smile on his face. "It's my little guy."

Clair tried to pull him back. He stopped four feet from the cage.

"Pike, step back." He turned to Clair, giving her a reassuring smile. "He knows it's me, I can feel it."

Just like, that the volt flattened into one long strand and extended all the way to Pike, slashing his suit and cutting him deep on his arm. Pike snapped out of the happy feeling. "Ouch! Yeah, that's him. Temper tantrum again."

The little volt started to turn pink, then became red and dripped out of the cage like blood. Clair grabbed Pike's arm, backing him up as they all watched the pool of blood pool. It bubbled and grew. They exited the lab and watched from behind glass. Clair saw Pike's cut heal right in front of her eyes.

Out from the blood grew a skeleton. Skin spread and covered exposed tissue. Next came hair follicles. A penis grew. Then facial features formed.

All mouths hung open.

The newly formed body moved clumsily at first, knocking into the slab and falling over. Standing unsteadily, he brushed back the long hair that covered his face.

He turned facing, facing the group.

Clair gasped, "Pike?!"

Clones you can't pick them

PIKE'S HEART RACED in disbelief. There was a clone . . .. A clone of himself. A naked fully formed clone of himself.

He turned his head to find Clair slack jawed.

"Stop staring at my willy!"

She slowly moved her gaze to him. "I . . . I . . . I'm not!"

He brushed past her. "Where's a towel? A sheet? Anything for the poor guy."

Pike unzipped his jumpsuit and shuffled out of it. He approached with caution. "Hey fella, why don't we get you dressed? You must feel cold."

New Pike watched what Pike was doing and started to mimic him. He hunched over with his hands out. Clair flew to the door. "Be careful. That is an aggressive stance."

Pike stopped. New Pike also stood still, wearing a matching expression. Somewhere between bewildered and terrified, Pike could feel that familiar, fuzzy warmth growing inside of him. He smiled. New Pike smiled. Pike straightened up and New Pike did the same.

Clair stepped forward cautiously and Pike's smile broadened. New Pike smiled wide to match him and turned to look at Clair.

She shook her head. "Oh, Jesus."

Pike made a hand gesture warning Clair to stay back and New Pike copied him.

Pike focused on his twin. "Hey, little buddy. We need to get you dressed." Clothes. He tugged at his cloths. New Pike tugged at his skin, but it wasn't coming off the way Pike's clothing was. New Pike reached down to the thing hanging between his legs and gave a tug. He smiled.

Pike overreacted. "No. No. No! Don't do that."

Clair held in a laugh and New Pike matched the concerned expression he saw on Pike's face.

Pike sighed. "Sorry, fella. It's okay. You didn't do any wrong." He held out the jumpsuit and stepped closer. New Pike held his hands outward as Pike approached. They were a few feet apart.

Pike let go of the jumpsuit with one hand and new Pike watched. "Hi buddy."

New Pike mimicked everything Pike was doing. They touched hands. New Pike's body temperature was much warmer than Pike's. "You're hot, buddy."

He turned back to Clair. "He's hot. Is he okay? Maybe he's running a fever."

Clair asked calmly, careful to make no sudden movement, "See if he can talk."

Pike nodded. "Good idea."

New Pike was nodding along. Pike spoke directly to him, "Hello."

New Pike watched Pike's mouth form the letter O as he finished the word. Clair stepped to the side, watching. "Is he going to kiss you?"

Pike narrowed his eyes and looked back at her. New Pike shot her a duplicate glare. "Oh, for the love of God."

"I should name him!" Pike turned to face New Pike. "Pike Jr., Pikester, Half Pike." Pike laughed. New Pike laughed. "I've got it. Adam!"

Clair huffed. "Like Adam and Eve?"

Pike and New Pike shook their heads. "No. It's my middle name."

She tried it out loud. "Pike Adam Evans. Adam. I like it."

Glancing back at the three scientists she made a *psst* sound to Pike. Adam liked that noise and stepped past Pike on his way to Clair. She did it again and this time turned to look at Pike. There was Adam walking toward her, penis swinging side to side.

"*Psst . . . . Bahahahaha!*" She blushed and covered her mouth. Adam stopped. Pike walked over and touched his arm. "Adam, come over here."

Clair's eyes watered as she fought to keep in her laughter. Adam liked the sound of her laugh and he covered his mouth, trying to push out a sound.

"Jesus, stop it, Clair. He sounds like he's being murdered."

She regained control and walked closer to them. Adam was clearly not a threat.

"Isn't it odd that the scientists are just standing there like this is no big deal?"

Pike watched demeanor. "What a minute. Yes. Do you think this has happened before?"

That got the attention of the closest member of the group. "Correct, Mr. Evans. As a matter of fact, this has happened several hundred times over the past decade. The longest-lasting specimen has survived six hours before imploding."

Another scientist pointed to Adam. "We were hoping it would stay in its energy form. Neumann really wanted this one."

Pike's heart sank. "He's going to die?" He turned back to Adam, trying to bring sound out. "No."

Clair wasn't sure what to think. "So, they reconstruct as a human and then drop dead?"

All three men nodded agreeing. "The first few times we experienced it was like a miracle," the third man said. "Now we time them."

Pike wasn't ready to hear anything about Adam dying. He was going to keep him alive. He quickly helped Adam into the suit.

"Clair, he's cooling off! Go get my other set of clothes from the truck. We have to keep him alive."

She nodded and ran out of the room bursting through the exit doors and running all the way to the truck.

The entire team watched her curiously. Jackson called out, "What's going on?"

She grabbed Pike's bag and threw it over her shoulder. "A new set of urgency. Got to get something to Neumann and hope it doesn't die on us."

Cooper was calling Clair as she met up with 49 in the hall. She motioned him to follow. "We have it," she told Cooper. "It's taken on a human form. The Three Amigos say they haven't had one last more than six hours."

"That truck was made for this. It has to ride in the trailer. I have a theory. We need to keep regenerating it."

"Him," she said. "Regenerating him. Congratulations, it's a boy."

49 stopped her. "What the hell is going on?"

She stood, anxious. "See for yourself. You're never gonna believe it."

Clair motioned for 49 to enter. Hanskon stepped away from the wall and behind her. "Not him." She pointed to Hanskon, "What the fuck, Clair?"

Clair tried to prepare 49 as they briskly walked to the end of the clean, white corridor. "Just go with it."

He was in the middle of asking for more information, but stopped cold upon seeing a trio of scientists laughing at Pike trying to put pants on a naked clone of himself.

49 stood, speechless. Clair touched Adam. He smiled.

All of Pike's frustration washed away. "Clair, he smiled. On his own. He smiled. Adam, good boy."

Clair unpacked Pike's personal belongings. "Lie down." She pointed to Pike.

"What?"

"He mimics you. Lie down. It's going to be easier to dress him."

49 stepped closer. "Never in all my years."

Pike touched Adam. "Okay, little buddy. We're going to lie down. Now watch me."

Pike lowered himself to the ground and Adam followed.

Clair gave orders for the next sequence. "Lift your legs and spread them a foot apart." Pike nodded. Adam followed. Clair slipped on his underwear. "Feet touching the floor, now lift your butt." Pike did it and so did Adam.

Pike grinned. "Good job, son. What's next, Clair?"

She secured the underwear in place and stared at him. "You're killing me. Really?"

Adam was fully dressed. The scientists took notes and complimented Clair on her tactics. She turned, muttering, "Idiots. I'm surrounded."

Pike was excited to see 49 and even more excited to introduce him to Adam. "Adam, this is your granddad."

49's eyes widened and his brows shot straight up. "Wait a minute. I've never sired a human in my life."

Pike and Adam grinned. "Well, you *are* the head honcho of our little team."

Clair spun on her feet. "Hang on."

Pike spoke softer so only Adam could hear, "and that is mom. Sorry she's a little cranky." Then, speaking up, he said, "But good news. We're taking you on a road trip. Might as well learn your family's roots."

No one knew where to look. Pike had lost it. This was no fantasy. They were on a mission.

Clair grumbled, "He's nuts." She played along, patting Adam's arm while overexaggerating her facial expressions. She couldn't believe the mess they were in.

"Sweetheart stay with grandpa while mommy has a word with daddy." She marched Pike over to the other side of the room.

"Ouchee! Ease up woman, our son is watching."

She released his arm. "Six hours. They said the longest one of these survived was six hours. We don't need a whole fill-in-the-blank fake family narrative attached to this. I get it that he's your clone. I can see why you want to protect him. But come on, this is cargo. We need to move it from Point A—meaning this god-forsaken tunnel—to Point B. Home base."

Pike turned pleadingly to 49. He and Adam rested one hand on each of 49's shoulders. Adam smiled adoringly.

"Look, I get it," Pike said. "But he was born from my DNA. That is my son. I have to do everything I can to keep him alive."

"That's not your son! That's your clone. It's the DNA of your parents." Clair studied him.

Pike didn't care how he was made or from whose ingredients he came from. Adam was his. He was invested. So was Clair, on a more reserved level. "Look, I spoke with Neumann. He said the truck is designed for this exact mission. He wants Adam alive, but here's the thing. Your boy has to travel in the back."

Pike didn't like this idea at all. "In the trailer part?"

She nodded. "Yup. He's hoping he survives the trip and has prepared accordingly to make that happen."

Pike blew out a breath that smelled like he needed to brush his teeth. She thought about that. They all did.

Clair stood with Adam. She taught him how to hug, figuring it was the best way to check body temperature. Adam learned quickly. He was a good hugger. She showed Pike. When Pike hugged him, Adam's temperature rose slightly.

Clair confirmed it, marking the temperature difference between contact with Pike verses contact with her. There was a five-percent change.

Clair marveled, "You're like a docking station."

"I don't care what I am. Adam needs to live. If I have to hold him the whole way there I will."

Clair agreed, if only to get them back on the road. Live or die, Adam was going with them.

Shell of the Unknown Cargo.

49 STATED THE OBVIOUS. "We have eighteen guys out there. How are we going to explain the clone?"

Pike corrected grandpa. "Adam. It's Adam."

49 pointed toward the door. So did Adam. "We load him like all the other cargo. I'll pull the trailer deeper into the tunnel and we load him so none of them can see."

Pike agreed. "Good idea. I still don't like the idea of him riding in the back. It's dangerous."

Clair ignored Daddy Pike. She circled her finger in the air. "Let's move him out."

49 backed to the dock where they would load Adam. Pike opened the trailer doors for the first time. There was a hospital bed in the center, blocked in with what looked like generators.

Pike was immediately on the phone with Cooper. "What am I looking at?"

Neumann gasped upon seeing Adam for the first time. "He morphed into you."

Pike smiled. "That's right. You haven't met junior yet. Cooper, meet my boy. I named him Adam."

"Fall of bliss. Interesting."

"My middle name."

"Oh. You shouldn't have named him. But I like the name Adam. We will keep it."

Pike didn't like how he said we. "The lab coats said they only got one to last six hours tops. How are you going to keep him alive?"

"See those boxes in there? They are energy packs."

Pike walked over and studied one. He squatted beside Adam, swatting his clone's hand away. "Don't touch. I don't know how this works yet."

Clair walked in. "We strapping him in?"

Pike stood, horrified as he saw the straps attached to the hospital bed. "No way. You are not restraining him."

She folded her arms. Adam folded his arms. Pike corrected him. "Don't copy mom."

"So you want him to be able to walk around freely? Like that's safe."

He ignored her for a moment and held up the phone. "Cooper, how do this work?" Lights illuminated the inside of the trailer.

"I have cameras in here," Cooper said.

Pike brought down his phone, sighing with relief. "Will I be able to watch him?"

"Yes, on the computer in the cab."

"Next to the bed?"

"Yes."

"*Phew*, good. Do we have to strap him in?"

"Yes. It's the only way to make sure the charge stays connected."

Pike didn't like the idea at all.

"The alternative is to bring him in the cab with you." Pike smiled, but 49 and Clair protested. Cooper continued, "At some point in the next few hours he will turn to dust. Your call, Pike."

Pike reluctantly agreed. "Fine."

Clair and Pike strapped Adam in. Pike made sure the straps weren't too tight. Just snug enough. He talked to Adam the entire time like he was calming a small child. Adam didn't seem to mind. He Just smiled while was he was being restrained.

Clair unfolded a padded blanket and used it to cover Adam. His smile vanished. Pike quickly pulled the blanket off. "What is this thing?"

Clair huffed out as Cooper's hologram appeared. "It's like the jumper cables to a car. It's safe. Feel it."

Pike felt the underside. A small burst of electrodes vibrated. It actually tickled. He gently pulled it onto Adam again. "It's okay, Adam. It won't hurt."

Clair watched Adam. "Is he sleeping?"

Pike grew worried. "Does he sleep, or is he dying? Am I losing him?" He shook Adam.

Adam opened his eyes and smiled. Pike stood, heaving out a breath, raking his hand through his hair. "Jesus, kid. Don't do that to me. Fuck."

Clair stared down, "He just needed a recharge. He's fine. Come on, you can watch him from the cab."

Pike knelt and reassured Adam. "Hang in there, little buddy. I'm going to take care of you."

A fracture of lightning twinkled in Adam's eyes. Pike whispered, "I will keep you safe." His heart beat strong. He was on a mission to keep Adam alive.

Clair stepped out from the back of the trailer. Hanskon was waiting there. "What the hell is going on? Why are you in there? We don't know what we carry. Why are you in there?"

Clair stepped to the side to block his path.

"What?" He reached out to touch her shoulder and she knocked his hand away.

"Don't touch me. I know it was you."

"Know what was me?"

"You hazed Pike."

"I don't know what you're talking about. What are you guys carrying that needs this much attention?"

"Don't worry about it. Just do your job."

"Clair."

"Fuck off." She marched past him.

He stepped to the back of the trailer and opened the door. His eyes found the hospital bed and the person strapped down. Pike was hovering over the body.

Hanskon walked in. "What the hell is this? Humans are not allowed to be transported like this."

He looked down at Adam. "Jesus. Who the fuck is that?!"

Pike's eyes narrowed. "Get the fuck out of here!"

"No, no, no! Is that your brother?"

"Something like that."

"Why is he in the back of this rig?"

"None of your fucking business. Leave."

49 stepped to the back of the truck. "Hanskon, get out of there. Not your business."

"Why are we transporting Asswipe's twin?"

"Classified. Get out."

"This is bullshit, man. No way am I protecting this shit."

"You'll do your job."

"I will protect my crew." He stormed past 49.

"Pike."

Pike looked up at 49. "Come on, kid, let's get her rolling. Adam will be fine. He's safe back here."

Pike looked down at his clone. "I will be right up there and I can watch you. So I am close, okay."

Adam smiled. Pike pulled up the weighted blanket. "Get some rest, little buddy. Cooper wants to meet you."

Pike walked out and sealed the doors. "Come on, let's get him to Cooper."

Rock a Bye Baby.

THE TEAM WAS READY. Clair announced they were coming out of the tunnel. Four Suburbans answered and moved out ahead of them, an occupant from each chiming out, "All clear," over the radio.

Clair pressed the talkie. "Copy that."

Green light lit the tunnel. Jackson was waiting at the entrance. "In position, Agent 50287.

"I see you," Clair responded.

"Copy that."

Jackson powered ahead. "Hanskon, wait to take up the rear position, then hang back."

They were out in the open. Pike watched the screen. "Clair, can you not weave as much? Adam's blanket is shifting. I don't want it falling off him."

Clair turned to 49. "What did he just say?"

"Never mind, just drive."

Pike called out for Cooper. His hologram lit the floor in front of the jump seat. "Cooper!" he called again.

Clair was getting annoyed. "He's here."

Pike peeked around the computer. "Oh, hey. Can his blanket come off?"

"How do you mean?"

"Like, from the way some of us drive."

Clair whipped her head around. "What?! You'd better not be referring to me."

Cooper reassured Pike. "It won't come off. It secures in place. I made sure of it. "

"Okay, good. Does he need any special food or water?"

The truck leaned slightly. "Easy!"

"Pike, ease up," Clair said. "We're going downhill on a steep curve. Go back to watching your baby."

"Fine. Coop, I'm going to call you. I have a load of questions."

Pike heard Jackson going over a driver check. "Looking good, team. Open road in twenty minutes. Stick together tight."

Nash's voice came over the radio. "Ten points for every blonde."

"Keep it professional, Yetis."

Five hours into the trip and it had been smooth sailing. Adam was still alive and Johnson's team confirmed it was ready to meet up at the next stop. The only problem was there weren't enough suits for the additional six guys.

Arguments broke out over the talkie. Johnson's crew demanded the Yetis give up their suits, but Jackson wouldn't budge. Instead, he decided his crew would stay on for the second leg of the journey. Johnson's B team wouldn't be necessary. There was no way Jackson and his men were giving up their suits.

Pike was on the phone with Cooper, asking about the other lifeforms that had come before Adam. He wasn't happy with what Cooper had to say.

Pike agreed Adam was stable for now and hung up, letting a huff out. He regarded how fast Clair was driving. "You can bump up your speed a little more. There's no one out here." He was ready to take over the next driving shift. If Adam died at this point, he didn't want to see it.

Clair's irritation spilled over. She couldn't stand the way Pike was behaving. "It's a damn good thing Jackie didn't get pregnant."

49 tried to stop her. Pike leaned in. "What does that mean?"

"It means you have been obsessed with . . . Adam."

"I . . . I . . . I can't explain it. I just know it's that same little guy from the plane. We made a connection back then. It's him trying to communicate. I want to know everything."

She softened. "Why did he morph into your clone?"

"I don't know. Maybe he's trying to relate and understand."

"Or confuse you and us so we don't kill him."

"No. It's something bigger. I feel it. I can feel it."

Pike had a point. Clair thought about that. Maybe she had gotten it all wrong with Pike. Maybe he wasn't under the clone's spell. Oh, sweet Jesus.

Up next was a fuel stop and clone check-in. 49 handled the fuel. Clair guarded the back while Pike checked on his clone. Adam was alive and happy. A relieved Pike tucked Adam back in and conferred with Cooper.

"He's one hundred percent on target, Pike," Cooper said. "Are you driving?"

He nodded. "Clair is going to monitor Adam."

Cooper interrupted. "She needs sleep. I will take over."

Pike protested. "But we're sitting right here."

"Trust me. I can detect something malfunctioning faster than you, even from here. I will give you plenty of warning if something is off."

Pike had no reason to question Cooper, but he didn't like the idea of anything going wrong either way. With each passing hour, Adam's life was a gamble.

Double Vision

THE ADAM CHECK-IN INSIDE the trailer was a success. Pike sat with him and soothed him. "We're going to get you safely to Cooper. Just hang in there."

Pike adjusted the weighted electro-blanket on Adam, making sure he was snug and the thing was doing what it was supposed to do. It zapped Pike, bringing back memories of his uncle's electric fence.

Adam's smile faded as he stared into Pike's eyes. Pike could feel it again. Something was there. Instead of happy feelings, Pike could feel a slight anger. He stood up, touching Adam on the shoulder. "It's okay, little guy. My fault."

Pike pulled his hand back. His brain raced and heart jolted. He had felt what Adam was thinking. Adam was upset that Pike had been hurt by the electric fence.

"Holy shit!" He stared at Adam, who looked happy again. "I'll . . ." he raked his hand through his hair. "What the fuck was that?"

He leaned over Adam. "You can feel that? Because I just felt that."

Clair banged on the back door. "Gotta roll."

Pike didn't know where to look. "I'm driving. You recharge. Cooper is sixteen hours away. If you hang in there, I promise I

will keep you safe."

Clair banged again.

"Adam, I mean it. I will protect you."

Warmth filled Pike. He knew Adam understood. "Gotta go, little buddy. Don't die."

Pike opened the trailer door. A few of the Yetis were hanging around. One in particular, Nash, walked alongside Pike. "I'm not even going to ask. Word on the street says you have an alien back there that looks like you."

Pike silently cursed Hanskon. Still, Pike liked Nash. He trusted him as well. "Who wouldn't want to look like me?"

Nash gave Pike a grave look. "It's true?"

"I'm driving this next shift. Try to keep up."

Nash reiterated, "Toe-to-toe, Evans. I have your six."

Pike looked stern. "This cargo is personal."

Nash understood and dropped the questions. "Like I said, I have your six."

Pike nodded. "Let's rock and roll, team."

49 took the passenger's seat. Clair secured herself in the jump seat and Pike leapt into the driver's position, adjusting the seat and commenting that they should invest in a booster seat for Clair. She was about to take it as an insult, but she could feel he was joking with her. She let go of her anger and relaxed.

Almost an hour on the road and pushing midnight, Clair asked Pike what she needed to look for while monitoring Adam before she got some sleep. Pike thanked her for the gesture as Cooper's hologram appeared. "Your services to Adam are not required. I have him monitored."

His dismissive tone rubbed Clair the wrong way. "Listen, buddy, I taught him how to dress. I have had contact. Don't you go ahead and tell me you have it covered. Pike, what am I looking for when I see him on the computer?"

"Well, the lights are on. You can watch him for a bit. Make sure the weighted blanket is on and there's not a pile of ash on the gurney."

Clair winced at that last comment. "Pike?"

He turned and she gave him a sympathetic look. "You're a good dad. You're going to be a good dad, someday."

He nodded. "Get some sleep. We need you alert if you're driving with Valentine."

She suddenly realized she would be the driver with him. "Lord, take me now."

49 lowered his cap over his eyes. "Wake me up in five hours."

Pike reminded him the bed above Clair was open, but 49 was happy where he was. Pike popped in his earbuds and started a playlist. It was time to cover some distance. Everyone took part in the radio check-in.

Big sky. Open road. Stars were twinkling. Pike looked up. They were unusually bright, actually. Maybe because it was because he'd been awake for so long?

Pike called over the radio. "Is it me or are the stars incredible?"

Jackson answered. "They're pretty awesome. Noticed it a few times lately."

An alarm sounded inside the cab. Pike's head pounded an instant before a bright flash blinded everyone. 49 searched the road as his vision returned and found that the trucks hadn't deviated in their speed or position.

Up ahead, the road looked like an inferno. Something had caught fire.

Clair staggered to the front. "What's happening?" A call for check-in came over the radio and Pike reported their status was fine. Everyone was okay.

Clair pointed ahead. "What is that?"

Cooper's hologram reappeared. "The system is down. Repeat, the system is down. I can't get any readings on Adam."

Clair zipped to the back. "I'll check the computer."

She reassured Pike, "He looks okay. His eyes are open. Oh, what are you doing? Adam, what are you doing?"

Pike frantically asked, "What is it? What is he doing?"

"Trying to sit up, I think?"

The fireball seemed to be getting closer, with chatter lighting up the radio... It looked like it was moving in the direction of the highway.

Pike tried tapping into the connection he had with Adam. Nothing. The fireball moved closer and Cooper's hologram became distorted, the audio scrambled.

Pike handed 49 his phone. "Get Cooper on this."

49 put Cooper on speaker. "Impossible. It's impossible! What's working in the cab?"

"Clair can see Adam. He's trying to sit up. We have a fireball heading toward the highway, ETA about five minutes. Your hologram is broken. I don't know what this rig does, but I have all my driving capabilities."

"Fire? What fire?"

Pike handed the phone to 49. "Show him what's ahead."

49 held the phone in place. "Neumann, I've never seen anything like this. It's not spreading. It's almost like it's walking."

49 tried to zoom in as much as he could without distorting the picture. Cooper watched, transfixed. The distance between them shortened. All at once, in the cab, over the talkie, and through the phone they shouted, "What the fuck?!"

The ball of fire was not spreading toward the highway. It was, indeed, walking. The vehicles started to slow and the flames came into better focus. It had legs, burning in orange, yellow, white, blue, and red. And it was walking right toward them.

Their convoy slowed. Jackson spoke over the talkie. "Treat this as a hostile. Someone get Cooper on the phone."

Pike grabbed the talkie. "He's on my phone. Our electronics are malfunctioning. I don't know how we're still communicating on this."

Cooper was on speaker. "Hanskon, Jackson, pull out those special cases I warned you about. We need to figure out how it's thriving."

Pike watched it move. Each step closer left a crater of smoke and ash in its wake.

Pike unbuckled himself. "I have to check on Adam. He's not going to die because of this douche."

Clair jumped out after him. They could hear thuds landing against the rear of the trailer. They scrambled onward to find the doors buckling under heavy blows from within. Everyone exited their vehicles in a panic.

Pike could feel the earth below his feet vibrate. He glanced down. Nash shouted out, "It's definitely heading our way.'

Jackson ordered everyone to secure their headsets. Pike hopped up on the back of the truck. "Adam, stop pushing the doors. You are damaging them. I am going to get you out, buddy."

Pike grabbed the handle and quickly retracted from the pain that seared his palm. His skin smoked and bubbled. Glancing back at the handle, he saw it was now starting to glow. Pike knew to jump back. He could feel the urge.

"Jesus, Adam, what are you doing?" The doors started to smoke. Clair ran back with their headsets and gasped. "He's going to burn in there."

Pike reached for her with his burned hand, The pain was already gone. "It's him. He's doing that."

He grabbed her with his other hand to hold her back while looking down at his damaged one. His skin rapidly repaired itself back to normal. "What the fuck?"

He thought he was losing it. He shook his hand. It had healed just like the gash Adam gave him. The right door danced with electricity and slowly opened, revealing Adam's hand pushing it. Electric currents hovered over his burnt skin. His clothes tattered. His eyes glowing.

The armored guys came charging in with their guns drawn. "What the hell is that?"

Adam looked like a singed version of Pike, who, along with Clair, held out his arms to the men in a panic, frantic to make them understand. "He's ours. Friend. Not enemy."

Clair urged, "Don't shoot him. He's ours."

Nash walked forward, staring at Adam, while Adam stood staring back at everyone. Pike went to him. White teeth. That's what everyone saw apart from the glowing white eyes. Pike motioned for Adam to come down. "It's a big jump, but if you squat down and sit." Pike made a sitting pose.

Morrison watched Pike. "Is he going to take a dump?"

Adam, keeping his eyes on Pike, stepped forward and fell to the ground face first. Pike leapt to him and felt a jolt of electricity surge through him when they made contact. A new round of panic spread through the group, and only Clair's shouts for the men to hold their fire kept control. Pike released Adam, his brain still buzzing from the jolts.

Jackson ran toward the back of the trailer. The whole crew felt the rumbling under their feet. Jackson struggled to make sense of what he was seeing. Adam was glowing face down on the road and Pike sat nearby on his bottom, looking confused.

Clair whipped around. "Everything is fine."

"Is that the freak Jon mentioned?"

She looked back toward Adam, whose skin was starting to regain its color as he pushed his body up off the ground. "That's our special delivery. Adam. He formed from a cut he gave to Pike. We need to get him to Cooper."

Adam regenerated his human form right in front of everyone's eyes. Nash put his hand to help Pike off the ground. "Maybe he could teach us all how to do that. Might come in handy after this shitshow."

Hanskon shouted, alerting everyone, "Walking thunder heading right for us. In position. What the fuck are you clowns doing?"

Jackson shouted out orders. 49, still on Pike's phone with Cooper, revved the tractor trailer engine and flipped the aux blue switch, lighting the whole rig up like a premier evening on Sunset Boulevard. There was a toggle controlling a beam of light aimed straight to the sky. Cooper guided him, and 49 fixed the beam directly on the flaming giant stomping their way.

Nash stared at the flames. "Fee fi fo fum, I smell the likes of a fire that needs extinguishing. Come on, men! Let's take back our ground."

They all moved to the front of the rig while the fire giant fought to escape from the beam of light.

Cooper fed instructions to 49, telling him to max out the engine's RPMs.

Pike called out, "What is he doing?"

Clair answered, "Saving all our asses."

The white light turned blue. The fire giant swatted frantically at the blue beam that bore into it. The fire burned red and black.

Jackson called in over the headset. "Whatever that thing is it looks like its starving the fire of oxygen. It's turning to coal."

Hanskon wasn't satisfied. He wanted this fucker, and a chance to test out the new weapon. He stepped forward, approaching the fire giant. "Fuck with the Yetis, and look what happens."

Eli shouted into the mic, "Stand down, Hanskon! Stand down. That is an order."

Hanskon ignored him, switching his laser gun on and aiming it right at the giant. A white beam shot from the gun and scored a direct hit. Hanskon's arms shook from the strain, though he wore a wild grin across his face.

49 shouted into the mic, "Stand down, you bastard. You're reversing the charge. Stand the fuck down!"

Two things happened. A burst of charcoal pelted the crew, and Hanskon disappeared.

Everyone ducked for cover and Pike held his ears to protect them from the screech of the giant glowing a newly intense white and yellow.

Alfie cursed into the mic. "I'm not going to die from electrocution. Not today. Not any day."

"Where's Hanskon?" it was Jackson's voice over the headset. "Has anyone see Hanskon?!"

49 revved the engine again, flipping another switch. The beast walked closer.

Jackson shouted, "On five, boys."

Nash took center, kneeling on the pavement with a device that resembled a rocket launcher. "Three, two, one." He shot a net over the top of the flaming giant.

The second crew took position. "Go!" They all charged and fired at the net, making the beast stumble backward to the ground. All the while, 49 continued to hit it with the blue light.

Still no sign of Hanskon. Clair looked worried. She left Adam and Pike, jumping into the truck with 49. She touched the windshield and looked for any sign of him on the grid. Smoke wafted from the giant as it again transformed to coal.

The guys watched the fire burn out. Jackson sounded hopeful, "It's working."

Smoke now billowed off the giant, which had lay motionless on the ground for the past half hour. Jackson, Pike, Adam, and several others approached the glowing embers.

Nash whispered from several yards away, "Ashes to ashes, dust to dust."

In a fraction of a second a bolt shot out of the smoldering giant and wrapped around Adam, then shot skyward and vanished. Pike watched in horror as Adam dropped to the ground.

The embers changed to black and Adam turned cold. Pike frantically picked Adam up and hugging him close. There was nothing there. No life.

Pike had to get him to the back of the trailer quick. He scooped up Adam in his arms and ran to the back of the trailer. Sirens approached in the distance as Jackson alerted them that the area was being secured.

They needed to get the cargo back to North Carolina, dead or alive. Clair wanted to stay to help search for Hanskon, but her brother refused.

Nash ran to Pike. "Let me help." He threw Adam's limp body over his shoulder as Pike jumped into the back. They hoisted Adam, and Nash climbed up to help move him into the hospital bed. Pike secured the weighted blanket, cursing, "Why isn't this working? What happened to the current? Why isn't this fucking thing on?"

49 appeared at the back and climbed in. "Pike, he's gone."

Pike shot a hateful look at 49, who repeated the words. "Son, he's gone."

Emptiness suffocated the hate. Pike couldn't feel him. Not their connection. Not anything. It was just a dead body. Pike's clone.

49 walked closer, trying not to look at the dead clone. "I am sorry, son. Truly sorry."

Nash stood and recited a prayer out load. Pike broke down and sobbed silently as his hands covered his face.

49 stepped over to his side and put an arm around him. "I know how you feel ,kid. I would be just as upset as you are if it were you." He held his arm tight around his shoulders as Pike tried to regain his composure.

Nash finished with an "Amen" and 49 repeated it. Nash walked around and cupped his hand over Pike's shoulder. "I've got your six, brother."

He glanced at 49, who relaxed his grip on Pike. "Thank you, Nash. That means a lot to us."

Clair jumped into the back of the trailer. She took one look at the clone, then at Pike. "Fuck this place. We need to make a delivery. I'm driving. Get in the cab. We are leaving."

Half the crew stayed to look for Hanskon. They were escorted by two Suburbans. Nash drove one and Jackson the other. There was no urgency other than to get home.

Clair, enduring on pure anger, insisted on taking the next shift. Pike stepped out of the tractor. "I'm up, I'll drive."

Jackson observed Pike's somber tone and overruled his sister, pulling rank. "He's driving. You go adjust your attitude. In back. On the sleeper."

She clenched her teeth, but climbed wordlessly into the truck. Jackson turned to Pike. "I'm sorry, man."

Johnson was ready for another encounter, all suited up and calling out formations.

49 topped the tanks and sealed the cap. "Come on, kid, we're sixteen hours away from home."

Johnson handed off to Valentine, who brought on a fresh driver for their team thinking they needed a break. 49 refused, telling Valentine his crew, of Clair and Pike would finish the job alone bringing in the rig. He needed to stick to guard duty escort. The two argued back and forth, eventually contacting Captain Jacobowski and letting her make the call. She had harsh words for 49, but sided with him in the end.

Clair looked wiped out. Even though she was still acting pissed off, her tear-stained, bloodshot eyes gave away that she had been crying not long ago.

It was nightfall again. Three hours away from Cooper's lab. Clair was driving and none of them had anything to say to the others.

Another hour passed. Clair cleared her throat. "I'm sorry about Adam."

Pike looked up from his phone. "Thanks. Sorry about . . ."

He couldn't say it and mean it. He hated Hanskon with every fiber of his soul.

Cooper's distorted hologram appeared again. "I am getting some extremely unstable readings. Prepare yourselves!"

A flash of light lit up the scenery around them and set off a sound like the back of the trailer blowing up. Clair gripped the wheel, steering out of the skid.

Cory shouted from the rear SUV to say the back doors had just blown open. Valentine led the patrol to the breakdown lane. Pike jumped out on the passenger side and ordered Clair to stay behind the wheel. He ran to the back doors to find them hanging half open. He clicked his flashlight on. The mist was thick in the back.

There was something small glowing. Oh, shit. Two sets of something small glowing. Cory hopped out from the Suburban with a better flashlight. He shined it in, standing next to Pike.

Adam was sitting up in the gurney smiling back at Pike. Cory moved the light to the right. There stood a naked Hanskon. Standing still. With glowing eyes.

"Fuck!" Cory shouted.

Pike climbed in and within a few feet tripped over a body. "Cory, what the fuck is that?"

Cory hopped in the back and directed the light on it. A body lay limp on the floor. Cory flipped it over. "Hanskon? Fuck, he's bleeding out!"

Pike's heart exploded with joy upon seeing Adam back in the body that had been dead for the past few hours.

Cory tied a tourniquet around Hanskon's arm and ran to the back of the trailer. "We need help! Man down."

Valentine found Cory shouting, "He needs to get to the hospital."

"Who?" he asked?

"Hanskon!"

Valentine's flashlight landed on the body on the floor. It was Hanskon, all right. He scanned from Pike to Adam and then to the Hanskon clone standing to the right.

Clair arrived, first spotting the naked Hanskon clone and then the body on the floor of the trailer. She leapt in, checking his vitals, as Cory held pressure on the gash. "He needs the hospital. Valentine, get in here and help us move him."

They had him out and in the back of the SUV in seconds. Clair insisted on going with him. No one was going to change her mind, as she held him protectively.

They were an hour away from Cooper's lab. Pike called Cooper, telling him that Adam was back and Hanskon was on his way to the hospital. Pike put both clones in the back of the cab. Pike was convinced Adam could survive and he didn't give a crap whether Hanskon made it.

He wrapped the Hanskon clone in a bedsheet and Adam stayed in his tattered clothes. They were ten minutes away from the Cooper's lab.

As 49 pulled into the hanger, Pike watched Adam and the Hanskon clone sitting side-by-side on the bed, smiling. *Fucking Hanskon. His genetically mutated body is just as chiseled as his human one.*

Finally, 49 pulled the tractor trailer in while the doors sealed behind it. Captain Jacobowski was waiting along with five other guys in lab coats.

Pike's phone rang. It was Clair. She was quiet. He spoke in her silence. "We just pulled into the lab. I've got to get these two out from the back of the cab."

"Pike."

He listened. "Clair?"

"He's dead."

Pike heard her take a sharp inhale. His heart sank a little for her pain. It was almost like he could feel it. "Clair, I am sorry."

He motioned for Adam to come out first. "Clair, I will call you in a bit. I've got to get these two out into the lab."

She hung up. He stared at his phone, torn between whether to call her back or get his clone out to meet Cooper. He chose his clone. Adam followed with complete understanding about how his limbs worked. He stood by the cab as the team of scientists approached.

Pike went back in to fetch the Hanskon clone, but he stumbled. He stumbled again, disoriented. His vision blurred and he could no longer see Hanskon sitting on the edge of the bed.

Pike fell to the floor as 49 shouted, "Stop! He's friendly!"

Pike turned over, barely able to move. The Hanskon clone leaned over and zapped Pike. It gave him a jumpstart, overriding what was happening. Pike focused. He felt drained.

49 scrambled into the cab. "Don't come out." They've taken Adam, and not in a nice way."

Pike was terrified, wondering what was happening to Adam. He looked at Hanskon. They didn't know about him.

Pike shoved him into the bathroom. "Stay here. I will get you to out and keep you safe. Everything is going to be just fine." Pike scrubbed his face, "Fack."

Don't miss out!

Visit the website below and you can sign up to receive emails whenever Suz Eglington publishes a new book. There's no charge and no obligation.

https://books2read.com/r/B-A-FPKX-LGXZC

BOOKS2READ

Connecting independent readers to independent writers.